BEYOND THE IVORY SHORE

❖ ❖ ❖

SAGAS OF IRTH
Of Swords and Sorrows
The Wrath of Shadows
The Night's Violin
Beyond the Ivory Shore
Upon the Serpent's Tongue
The Twilight Isle
Lady Midnight
The Song of the Sorians
The Iron Knight

SAGAS of IRTH · 4
Beyond the Ivory Shore
...
DANE VALE
NOSETOUCH PRESS
CHICAGO · PITTSBURGH

Beyond the Ivory Shore

ISBN-13: 978-1-944286-16-3

Published by Nosetouch Press
Chicago, Illinois 60611

www.nosetouchpress.com

Publisher's Note:

For more information, contact Nosetouch Press:
info@nosetouchpress.com

Cataloging-in-Publication Data
Names: Vale, Dane, author.
Title: Beyond the Ivory Shore
Description: Chicago, IL : Nosetouch Press [2021]
Identifiers: ISBN: 9781944286163 (paperback)
Subjects: LCSH: Fantasy — Fiction.
GSAFD: Fantasy fiction. | BISAC: FICTION / Fantasy.

To Kit, Key, Bean, and Dean—
you'll get there, yet!
❖ ❖ ❖

Table of Contents

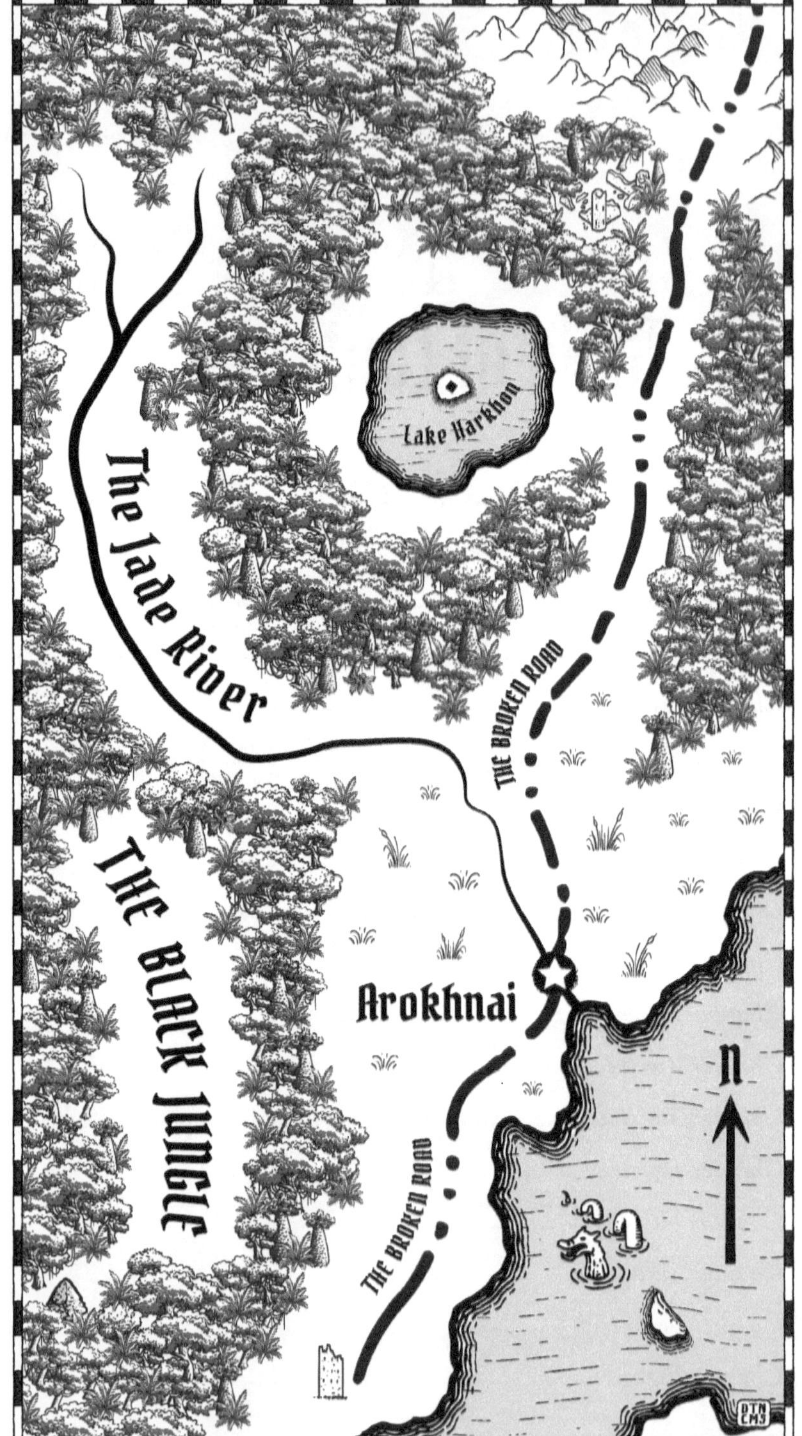

Lake Harkhon
The Jade River
THE BROKEN ROAD
THE BLACK JUNGLE
Arokhnai
THE BROKEN ROAD
N

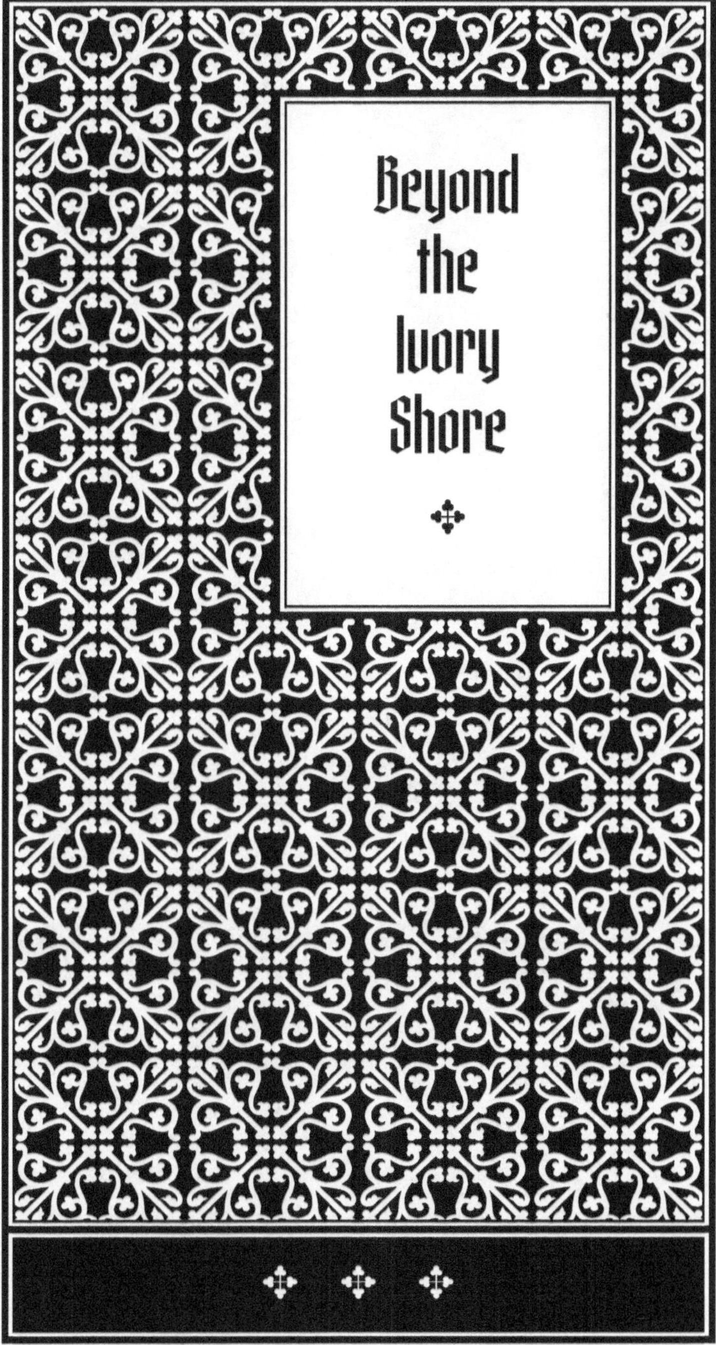
Beyond
the
Ivory
Shore

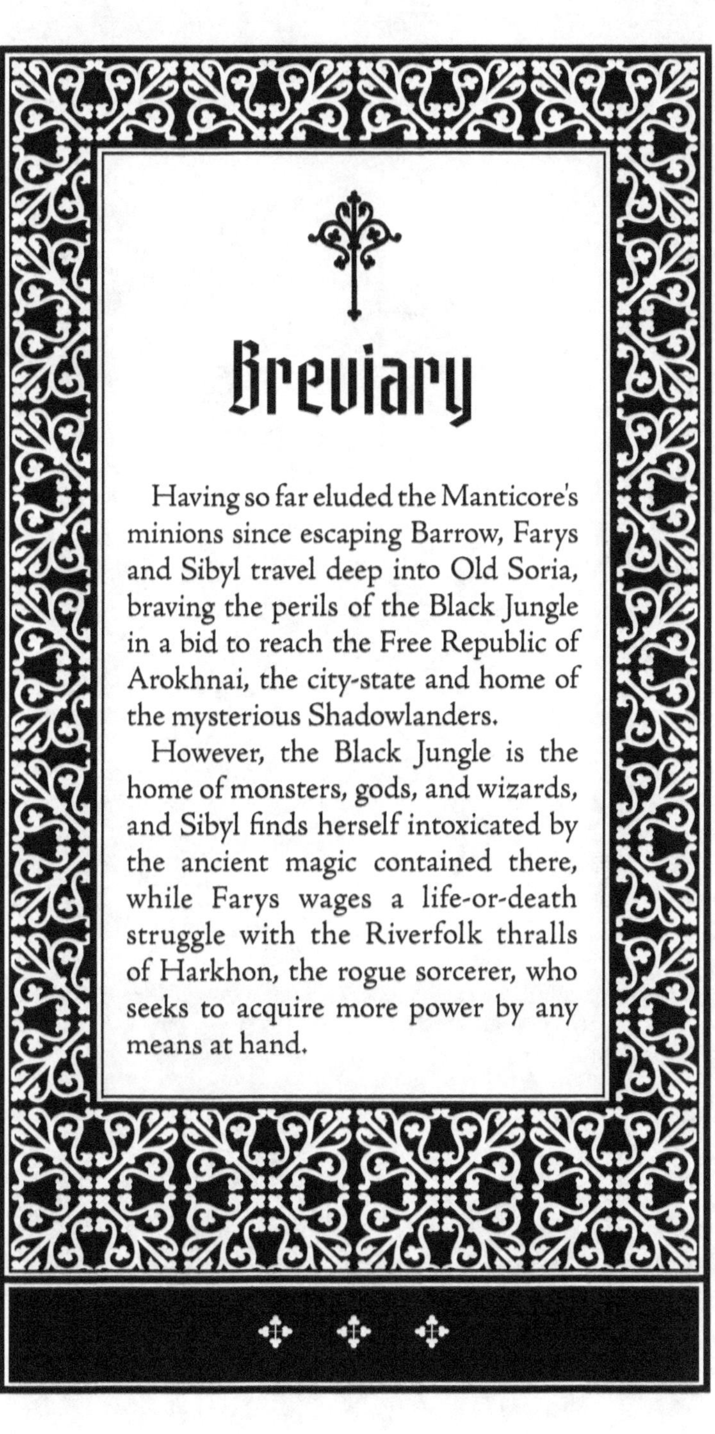

Breviary

Having so far eluded the Manticore's minions since escaping Barrow, Farys and Sibyl travel deep into Old Soria, braving the perils of the Black Jungle in a bid to reach the Free Republic of Arokhnai, the city-state and home of the mysterious Shadowlanders.

However, the Black Jungle is the home of monsters, gods, and wizards, and Sibyl finds herself intoxicated by the ancient magic contained there, while Farys wages a life-or-death struggle with the Riverfolk thralls of Harkhon, the rogue sorcerer, who seeks to acquire more power by any means at hand.

One

Two travelers made their way through the Black Jungle, beneath the shadow of massive mujandi trees, across the densely packed and drenched ground. Around them, the sun-sweltering canopy of trees steamed and dripped with moisture, with tangles of roots and poisonous shoots winding everywhere. A storm had passed through only an hour before, and they were both soaked by the deluge.

"For a place called the Black Jungle," the man said. "All I see is a sea of green."

The man, Farys, had cut his reddish hair short since their time in the north, and had stowed his armor with their long-suffering horses, which they led with care through the unforgiving undergrowth. He wore a white cotton tunic and a grey vest, with ash-blue breeches.

The woman, Sibyl, wore a bright red shift, having tied her golden tresses back with a black ribbon, her blue eyes scanning their surroundings.

"We are lost, Farys," Sibyl said. "Why travel overland this way?"

"We had little choice. Overland is the quickest, safest route for us to reach Old Soria. We can't risk travel by boat, which would require us to go around the continent itself, past your ancestral home, and in deadlier waters, still. This was the best route."

"It hardly feels like that," Sibyl said. "This Black Jungle carries the cries of the endless dead in its roots and branches."

"Does it?" Farys asked. He had enjoyed her theatrical, naturalistic musings on their long journey because, contrary to his own steely, cynical way with the world, he knew she had insights that were unavailable to him, and, therefore, potentially useful. Another perspective often made all the difference.

Her eyes flicked over him, trying to read his tone.

"And we're not lost," Farys said.

"No? Then where are we?" Sibyl asked.

"Heading south. As intended," Farys said.

"'Jungle' is a foolish word," Sibyl said. "There is no word for it in Mandrian."

"That's only because Mandria has no jungles," Farys said.

"If we did, we would have had a better word for them," Sibyl said.

"Do you really think so?" Farys asked.

Farys had rescued Sibyl many months earlier from the frontier town of Barrow, where she had been nearly hanged for witchcraft by the Manticore's minions. Barrow, like so many towns and cities in the Northlands, had fallen to the Manticore, the inhuman conqueror who was waging the Northwar. The two of them were effectively refugees, on the run for their lives from the Manticore and his assassins, set on vengeance.

"Yes," Sibyl said. "This jungle seethes."

"I think all jungles do," Farys said.

"Not like this," Sibyl said, stepping carefully through the wet foliage. While it was true that she had never seen a jungle before, she was certain they weren't all like this. This jungle was soaked with magic in a way she had not thought possible. To her eyes, everything shimmered with it. The energy of the place was undeniable, and irresistible.

"I couldn't find us a better route," Farys said. "There are old roads in this jungle we might take that should be easier to traverse. And, if we can reach the Jade River, we might have an easier time of it."

Farys had made it his quest to fight the Manticore and his acolytes, as repayment for the murder of his own family and the pillaging of his ancestral lands when he was a Borderlandish boy in the chilly north.

Although he'd left his life of knighthood far behind him, his desire for justice endured, and his efforts had earned him the nickname "The Wolf Knight" both for his chosen standard, and his reputation for ferocity and tenacity against the Manticore's followers. He had sworn revenge as a boy, and he would have it, no matter how many mercenaries and assassins the Manticore sent after him.

"A river would be welcome," Sibyl said. "This jungle is no place for us."

But where they were, the Northwar was thankfully far away, and the ride had been long and exhausting, avoiding the Leaguist cities, for fear of crossing paths with agents of the Manticore, who were known to infiltrate cities he aimed to conquer. As yet unconquered by the Manticore, the prosperous Free League cities would not welcome more refugees in their ranks. There were too many there, already.

Instead, Farys had taken them far south, toward Old Soria, with the Republic of Arokhnai, a fabled and ancient city-state, as their destination. Arokhnai was no friend of the Manticore's, and Farys had friends there who could help them.

"The Sorians watered this jungle with the blood of ceaseless sacrifices," Sibyl said. "The ground shrieks with it, even now, after so long."

Sibyl had run away from her home in Mandria, where a different—and, in so many ways, far worse—monstrosity ruled: the golden Dragon of Mandria.

For the Dragon, Sibyl had been a coveted prize who had slipped from his scaly clutches as a girl, risking everything to travel east into the wilderness, rather than become a slave-sacrifice, bound to serve the Dragon.

Farys saw her daub a bit of blood from her nose, and his flippant smile shifted a little. If there was Blood Fever about, they would both be in a world of trouble soon. The jungles of Soria were host to all manner of unknown diseases, with Blood Fever being one of the most notorious of them.

"Are you okay?" Farys asked.

"I'm fine," Sibyl said. "It's nothing."

"We're not so far from the White Towers of Arokhnai," Farys said. "We'll be there in a few days, I promise you."

"You said that weeks ago," Sibyl frowned. "What's there?"

"A friend," Farys said. "A good friend."

Farys minced the words as best as he was able. Arokhnai was a powerful place, and it was a free place. His friend, Fiss'Q, was a Shadow Warrior, who could surely help them. And, in the Southlands, powerful friends were good friends, indeed.

The Mandrian witch looked skeptical, grimacing as they made their way slowly through the dense underbrush.

"Must be some special friend," Sibyl said. "For you to go such lengths to see them."

"Oh, most certainly," Farys said.

"Why are we down here, Farys?" Sibyl asked, while Farys helped her ford a stream with her horse. Ordinarily, she would simply use the Sight she possessed to divine the answer, but there was something about this jungle that made her unwilling to do so. The potency of the magical energy around this place made Sibyl warier than usual.

"The Manticore came from here," Farys said. "I need to learn what it was he found that made him what he is, if I'm going to be able to kill him."

It was part of the lore of the Manticore that he had once been a wizard, before throwing off his human form and becoming the monstrous conqueror who fought the world and won himself a share of it through brilliant war-mongering.

Some bards and sages spoke of deals with demons, and others of a curse. Whatever had taken place had occurred in the heart of the Black Jungle. Farys meant to uncover his secrets, and to, perhaps, divine a way to defeat his life-long adversary.

"And that is why you bring me here?" Sibyl asked. "To discover the source of his power?"

"Well, for your delightful company, too," Farys said. "I do so hate to travel alone."

"You're making a joke," Sibyl said. Her voice carried with it the distinctive Mandrian lilt whenever they spoke the Mainland tongue. It was a curling, curving sort of way they had with words, at once forceful and furtive, like the Mandrians, themselves.

Farys had never really known a Mandrian before, had only seen them from afar. Sibyl had strong features, as was characteristic of Firstmen—big eyes, golden hair, a prominent nose and jaw. She stood out in the Northlands, as all Mandrians did. All Firstmen were proud folk. A Secondman, himself, he didn't think they were all that different.

From what he remembered learning as a boy, the Firstmen—Mandrians and the people of Stormfist—had never suffered the tyranny of the Sorians. The Secondmen had lived in the monstrous shadow of Soria. That lingering fear clung to the hearts of all Secondmen, a great fear and hatred of tyranny, lest the dark heart of Soria beat again and enslave them all again.

"I may be joking, but I mean it, too," Farys said. Sibyl glanced at him, their eyes meeting a moment.

"Which part?" Sibyl asked. "Which part is the joke?"

"All of it," Farys said. "Never mind."

"I'm no joke," Sibyl said.

"That is very true," Farys said.

"'Joke' is another stupid word," Sibyl said. "It's not funny."

Farys laughed at that, and, after a moment or two, Sibyl laughed, too. Their laughs rang out amid the trees and vines, in the cacophony of the jungle.

They cleared the stream and were on an overgrown and broken Sorian road, intertwined with tenebrous vines as thick as their arms.

"At last," Farys said. "The Broken Road. This leads to Arokhnai."

The road cut southeast, by the Wolf Knight's estimation. They let the horses drink, while he and Sibyl rested a moment. The witch's blue eyes scanned the canopy around them, the wet-scented air from a thousand monsoons. Her eyes were getting bloodshot, and she daubed her nose again for blood.

"This is a cursed place," Sibyl said. "Every part of it screams its pain. I See it, whether I want to or not."

Farys listened for a moment, shrugged. "I can't hear it."

"You don't have to hear it to know that it is there," Sibyl said. "As a girl, I heard stories of a monstrous forest. The things that walked and shambled within it: Sorians and far worse. It was probably this place."

In the time of the Sorian Empire, the Iron and Black Jungles had been the very seat of Sorian power, with their cities built along the coasts, and astride the great rivers. It was unknown whether the jungles spawned the Sorians, or whether they corrupted the jungles themselves with their blood magic to feed their monstrous appetites.

Whatever the case, they were tainted by the blood magic of Soria, even long after the collapse of their empire at the hands of the Preserver and the gods of the North, who had delivered the apocalyptic plague that had ended them millennia before.

All around them, there were cries of birds and other things. Ahead of them, on the Broken Road, appeared a man out of the mists.

He was as tall as Farys, but leaner by far, and wore a robe of yellow. His face was gaunt to the point of being nearly skeletal. His honey-hued hair was braided across his scalp, and he wore several necklaces of polished amberwood beads, which hung around his slender neck. His

eyes were black and rimmed with kohl, and his hands were bare, twitching clawlike at his sides. He bore tribal tattoos upon his cheeks, in the form of tumbling triangles rendered in black ink. The man also had a pair of black tears tattooed at the corners of either of his eyes.

"You!" the man said, his voice high-pitched, almost keening. "Who are you to dare to travel alone upon the Broken Road to Arokhnai?"

"I'm Farys of Foxbridge," Farys said. "This is Sibyl of the Red Mountain."

"The Red Mountain," the man said, cursing. "I am Harkhon, Magus of the Broken Road."

Old Soria was filled to overflowing with crazed magi, scavenging the lost magic of the Sorians, hermit-scholar-wizards who plied the ruins and risked the perils of the jungles for even a hint of the powerful treasures within. They came from all over Irth, seeking power in the shadow of the devastation of Soria.

"We are honored to meet you, O Great Magus," Farys said, giving him a gentlemanly bow. He had found in his travels that it behooved one to be courteous to magicians. Sibyl, for her part, was far less than impressed, looking at Harkhon down the end of her bloody nose.

"You call yourself a magus," Sibyl said. "But what can you do?"

"You doubt me, Witch?" Harkhon said. "This is my place, and any who travel upon it must pay my toll."

"Foolish skinny madman," Sibyl said, stepping forward to confront the magus, who stood his ground upon broken pavestones. "What is your price for passage, Secondman?"

"Secondman?" Harkhon said, angered at the word. "Mandrian trash!"

Farys rested his hand on the hilt of Tempest, his mermaid-hilted rapier and one of his favorite swords, while Sibyl faced down the magus, who appeared undaunted in the face of the Mandrian witch.

"I have no need for gold sovereigns upon the Broken Road," Harkhon said. "No need for finer things. I would seek something else, instead."

The magus produced a bamboo flute with three pipes bound tight with dried bloodvine, and he sounded it, the three dissonant notes sharp and clear, and, at once, three dozen tribesmen emerged from the undergrowth of the jungle, bearing bows aimed at the two travelers.

Farys could see the orange sap that tipped the arrows the tribesmen aimed at them, and coughed, catching Sibyl's eye.

"Poison tips," Farys said. "Oh, I don't like that at all."

Harkhon grinned at them, his teeth stained red by the berries of some infernal fruit of the Black Jungle.

"Heed the wisdom of the Wolf, Witch," Harkhon said.

"Brigand," Sibyl said, as the tribesmen moved in and surrounded them. They were all young men, their skin the color of pale jade, dusted with a white powder-paint that made them look even more feral than they already were. Their eyes were reptilian, and their countenances were like cold stone, as they approached and disarmed Farys. At the careful urging of Harkhon, they tied Sibyl's hands behind her. They bore beaded necklaces of ivory and ocher, from which a lone, large polished whitestone teardrop depended.

"Rivermen," Farys said, prompting a laugh from Harkhon.

"O Worldly Warrior," Harkhon said, mockingly. "To know of such things."

The Rivermen hunted and haunted the banks of the Jade River, where they preyed on anything they could get their hands on. Something more than bandits and less than pirates, they were known for their almost mystical savagery, and their fearlessness. How Harkhon had managed to get them to do his bidding was something Farys could not, as yet, determine.

Harkhon held Tempest in his hand, turning the beautiful blade this way and that, admiringly.

"This is a fine sword," Harkhon said. "Not from around here."

"It's very special to me," Farys said. "Be careful with it, though, it's sharp."

Harkhon laughed, waving it about, gesturing with it.

"Now, we go someplace interesting," Harkhon said.

Two

Harkhon took Farys and Sibyl to a clearing in the jungle, a bone-white beach that surrounded a great volcanic lake, where an island stood at the center. On that island was an ancient whitestone temple that was devoid of foliage, which set it apart from everything else in the area.

The temple was a large ziggurat that was meticulously carved by a craft that was far beyond the abilities of the Jade Rivermen who hauled Farys and Sibyl to the shores of the lake. The alien nature of its design, its cyclopean motifs spoke to its Sorian design. Whatever its purpose in antiquity, it had a new purpose, now, at the hands of Harkhon of the Broken Road.

When they reached the banks of the lake, which was a milky sky blue in hue, Harkhon gestured and had his captives take a seat on the blinding white sand. The heat of the day was almost overwhelming, and everyone was sweating.

Then he gestured, and his Rivermen began to light a great bonfire, and to caterwaul and dance at the shore.

"Longmaw," Harkhon said, gesturing at the temple that loomed in the distance. "For you, Wolf Knight."

"We were heading to Arokhnai," Farys said, prompting Harkhon to scoff.

"Arokhnai? What shadowy business have you there, Wolf Knight?" Harkhon asked. He watched the Rivermen clear their horses of gear, unsheathing the knight's seven swords and stabbing them into the white sand around the magus, who looked on them with delight and greed.

"Not slaving, Ansiblean," Farys said, but the magus interrupted him.

"I left Ansible a lifetime ago, Borderlander. Perhaps I should sell you to the slavelords of Uriokh," Harkhon said, plucking lovely Tempest from the sand, the green rapier's blade radiant in the light of the beach. "You could spend the rest of your days rowing one of their war galleys, fight for your life in their Bloodgarden, or serve as an anchor in the Bay of Boundless Sorrow for the amusement of your new masters."

"Not how I was planning to go, to be honest," Farys said, prompting the magus to clap his hands. Several burly Rivermen grabbed Farys and dragged him to a canoe, which they boarded, shoving off for the island.

"Don't try to swim the water, Wolf Knight," Harkhon said. "It is poison."

Farys winced at the sight of the water, and glanced at Sibyl, who looked on with veiled concern. The whites of her eyes were very red, now, and blood ran down her face. Despite this, and the evident pain she was feeling, she was otherwise okay.

"What is happening to him?" Sibyl asked.

"Sacrifice to Longmaw," Harkhon said. "Don't you see? This place is sacred."

Sibyl gazed across the blue-white water, and the bone-white shore, and the tower on the island.

"Sacred to whom?" Sibyl asked.

"To Longmaw, of course," Harkhon said, as if it were obvious. He cut the air with Tempest, this way and that, back and forth. "Green steel. Adamantine and something else. Something old. Something Sorian. Light and lethal. Is it his favorite blade?"

The magus stabbed Tempest into the sand, before grabbing another, a Wildland saber, from which hung a black braid and a half-dozen coins.

"He has many favorites," Sibyl said. "He's deadly with them all."

"Bah," Harkhon said, watching the canoe recede toward the island, swinging the saber about with whistling cuts at unseen adversaries. "It matters not. He's but a swordsman. We can speak of far finer things, you and I."

He traced an arcane rune in the white sand with the saber, and gave Sibyl a sidelong glance.

"I have nothing to say to you, Magus," Sibyl said.

"But you will," Harkhon said. "Soon enough, you will. You bleed. The blood magic makes you bleed. Strong, indeed."

Harkhon snapped his fingers, and the Rivermen set upon the pair of horses, slaughtering them with cuts of wooden swords edged with obsidian, the blades of white-wood and volcanic glass easily cutting the horses' heads off, sending the hapless animals falling to the white sand, staining it red with their blood. Their dying shrieks filled Sibyl's ears.

"More blood for the blood magic," Harkhon said. "Blood for the soil, for the sleeping gods of Soria. Blood awakens them."

The magus looked on with glee, while his Rivermen flayed the horses, cutting meat from them, spearing it and putting it over the fire to roast.

"Farys will kill you for slaying his horse," Sibyl said. "He was very fond of it."

"Ha," Harkhon said. "Serves him right, bringing horses to the Black Jungle."

"I despise this place," Sibyl said. "It is toxic."

"You will think differently when you are here for a time," Harkhon said. "Everything is stronger, here. Magic is stronger. When I first came, my nose bled, like yours. It did. But I grew stronger. It flows through me, now. You know magic. I *am* magic. The Sorians live on in the jungles with us. They whisper secrets in my dreams."

Sibyl gazed at the dark eyes of Harkhon with open loathing. She'd never encountered a magician before. They were most common in the Leaguist cities, where they could pursue their magic relatively unmolested by great lords. The stories were told of great wizards, but she cared nothing for them. Whether taught in Valdikan or Ansible, the path of a magus was not the path of a witch. And this Harkhon was not a great man.

"Secondman," Sibyl said. "You are a pretender to the splendid arts."

"Pretender?" Harkhon asked, his dark eyes afire, as his Rivermen tossed the remains of the horses into the porcelain blue of the volcanic lake. The sun was all but blinding. "You think I am a pretender, Mandrian?"

"I See that you are," Sibyl said, brushing away the glyph Harkhon had drawn in the white sand with a sandaled foot. The magus glowered at her.

"Secondman I may be, but so is your Wolf Knight," Harkhon said. "You Firstmen and your pestilential arrogance. You are not so proud now, are you, Mandrian?"

The scent of cooking horseflesh filled the air, and Harkhon clapped his hands, the Rivermen taking out drums and beginning to pound out a beat that filled the air around them. The drumbeats were almost mesmerizing, like a thousand heartbeats. Riverwomen emerged from the jungle brush, looking like their menfolk, their long hair in serpentine braids that coiled around their shoulders. They carried small drums as well, and had the same reptilian eyes, devoid of warmth and compassion.

Sibyl watched the Rivermen and Riverwomen sway and pound their small drums of cinnabar hue, like countless little thunderclaps that sounded across the bright blue lake.

Farys could be seen in the distance, standing on the island. Sibyl could see the Wolf Knight on the shore before the white temple, with a spear, while the Rivermen paddled back, without a backward glance.

"Your Secondman will die on the island, like all the others," Harkhon said. "Longmaw will make short work of him, and you will have nothing left but to throw yourself on the white sand and beg me for forgiveness at your insult."

Sibyl was undaunted, looked the magus in the eye.

"Show me your wizardry, Secondman," Sibyl said. "Show me what you can do."

Harkhon stabbed the Wildland saber into the sand with a feral growl, drawing up another blade, a short sword made of auri, the rose-gold metal forged by the Dwarves. He tested it in his hands, felt the weight of the thing, approved of it. Auri was a magical metal, both light and strong.

"You will sing another song when your Secondman is devoured by Longmaw," Harkhon said. "Longmaw no longer needs to eat. Now, He eats only because He wants to. We feed Him sacrifices, and He is pleased."

Sibyl gazed out at Farys, so far away on the island, and, as her eyes reddened with blood, she wished for his gods to protect him.

Three

farys watched the Rivermen row off, marveled at the
rousing sound their drums made from across the poisoned water of the lake. They had left him a spear, had
said something to him in their bastard tongue, with only
the words "Longmaw" evident.

He regretted having taken Sibyl along the path they'd
traveled. The last time he'd ventured in the Black Jungle,
there had been no Harkhon of the Broken Road; there
had only been the Broken Road to Arokhnai, itself, and
Fiss'Q had been with him. It had been years ago.

Farys turned his eyes upon the white temple, which was
startlingly free of jungle vines. The whitestone of it was as
pure and white as if it had been bleached by lime, as if it
had not been ancient before the world was born.

The sculpture of it was arcane. It looked like anything
the Sorians had made—both enduring and profane.
Their sculptors could hew even the strongest of stone, using muscular might and blood magic to create whatever
shapes they required in their temples, monuments, and
cities.

As enamored as they were with their blood magic, the
Sorians were particularly fascinated by stonework. Their

handiwork—and the handiwork of their slaves—filled Old Soria. Although he seldom thought about them, seeing the temple here, Farys wondered what the world looked like when the Sorians were alive. Even the ghosts of that past in the Slaver Cities were impressive.

The lake of blinding blue was no different. With his understanding of Sorian antiquity, Farys assumed that Harkhon intended for him to be sacrificed to whatever lived within the temple. The sculptures did not speak to the occupant, only revealed a plethora of half-human and Sorian figures intertwined, communicating all manners of architectural obscenity in another of the carnal preoccupations of the Sorians.

Gazing around the little island, which, flanking the temple, contained a few great mujandi trees and plentiful crushed and broken bones, some fallen tree branches, and well-worn stones. Nothing more.

Across the water, he could hear the chant of the Riverfolk, over and over: "Longmaw! Longmaw! Longmaw!"

Farys moved to the edge of the temple, the arched entrance, which led into a place of deathly darkness, from which a strange scent emerged—something like strayfruit soaked in brandy and creosote.

That they had left him a spear felt almost like an insult, and he tested the tip, finding that it to be etched stone, not the obsidian they'd used for their blades. He hadn't used a spear since he was a boy, first learning some of the knightly weapons of his father and brothers. Farys tested the spear in his arm, found it to be strong amberwood, with the necessary tensile spring wedded to sturdiness.

For what it was worth, it was a good spear, and not a ceremonial one, as he had feared.

"Longmaw! Longmaw! Longmaw!"

The temple within looked to be a kind of cistern, containing not the blue-white water of the volcanic lake, but clear water, of undetermined depth. Glancing upward, Farys could see that the temple tower was itself porous—the endless, intertwined statuary honeycombing and allowing little beams of light within the broad, low floor of the place.

Massive white columns traveled down the length of the temple, and still, no moss or mildew grew. He could see a stone ramp led from the watery floor to his own position at the lip of the temple.

"Longmaw! Longmaw! Longmaw!"

Farys had no desire to step into the temple. Indeed, he feared that if he did, he'd simply slide within its uncertain depths, unable to escape. It was like so many of the deadly plants in the Black Jungle, capturing and killing prey in lethal pitcher traps, or in great, snapping jaws.

The tribal drums kept beating, the Riverfolk kept chanting, and somewhere in the shadowy depths of the temple, something dreadful stirred.

The contrast between the blindingly bright light outside the temple and the dappled darkness within could not be more pronounced. Farys squinted into the shadows, watching the water in the temple ripple as something moved within it.

"Longmaw! Longmaw! Longmaw!"

There came a great grunting sound, something throaty and powerful, echoing within the stone walls of the temple. Following that, a monstrous splashing noise, as the hellish beast within stirred and worked its way from its lair to the floor of the temple.

Farys recoiled at the sight of the creature, emerging into the beams of light. It was a massive thing, broad-headed, easily the width of four horses, and its great head was smooth and white in hue, like the white of the temple, and of the beach.

It had no eyes Farys could see, but its wide mouth was filled with teeth that were easily the size of the Wolf Knight's hands. They were triangular and smooth, and the beast let out a thunderous bellow that stilled the drums and the chanting of the Riverfolk.

Past the great head of the thing was a pair of muscled arms that were like pillars, ending in clawed, flippered hands that splashed explosively with each dragging step. The rest of the body of the monster was sinuous and long, ending in a lengthy, flapping, finned tail.

Somehow, the beast detected Farys, as it thumped toward him across the water of the temple-lair, a sickening, jarring step-step-slide as it made its way in his direction, uttering its trumpeting roar that was deafening at this range, amplified by the stone around it, like the echoes in a cave.

Farys stepped back from the lip of the temple, instinctively moving out of reach of the monster. That move saved his life, as the thing shot its tongue out at him—a massive, pinkish column of globular flesh striking the air where Farys had been standing only a moment before, smacking wetly against the whitestone at the edge of the temple.

The creature reeled its great tongue back in, roaring anew, and dragging itself toward the ramp.

Cursing, Farys quickly sidestepped out of the entrance of the temple, grateful to Fortune that he'd moved when he did.

Then, he began to climb the temple tower, taking advantage of the endless erotic protuberances of the Sorian sculpture. He did this, even as the monstrous Longmaw worked its way out of the entrance of the temple, visible now upon the ivory shore of the island.

At the sight of it, the Riverfolk let out a terrified and exultant cheer, and began chanting his name again, over and over, with even more passion and ferocity.

"Longmaw! Longmaw! Longmaw!"

Farys was not sure how he could hope to survive long on this tiny island with the gargantuan thing that was hunting him.

Four

"You see?" Harkhon asked. "See how your Secondman flees from mighty Longmaw?"

Sibyl was revolted at sight of the monstrous beast that slither-dragged its way from the temple. It was so much larger than Farys, and was aggressively hunting him.

The creature repulsed her, even from this distance. Its snow-white and glistening body was repellent to her, like a great maggot-worm, or a cave fish. In the hard light of the Southland sun, the thing was blindingly bright.

"What is that?" Sibyl asked, curling her lip in disgust.

"It is the temple god," Harkhon said. "There are so many gods in Soria. More than you could count. They all have their temples. One day, I shall have my own, just as Longmaw does. I already have my followers. Soon, they shall worship me, just as they do Longmaw. We will form the Pantheon of the Broken Road."

Sibyl was outraged at the hubris of the Secondman magus, who leered at her, oblivious to her anger, lost in his dreams of godhood.

"And you will help me get there," Harkhon said. "With your magic wedded to my own. I will become far more than I already am."

"I will do no such thing," Sibyl said. "I have not seen it."

Harkhon laughed. "You hold yourself so high, Soothsayer. As if that were the grandest of magic. I am stronger, still. Your Sight might have impressed me as a boy in Ansible, first learning the art. But I have lived in the jungles for years. I have seen wonders beyond the realm of dreams."

Sibyl wondered how Harkhon could perceive her Sight, but assumed his own saturation with the blood magic of the jungle had imbued him with that ability to perceive what might not be apparent to others.

Harkhon held out his hand for her to see, like he was performing a magic trick, and conjured flame that danced upon his open palm, without burning his flesh. Some of the nearby Rivermen, who were intently watching Farys content with Longmaw, saw the display of fire from Harkhon and backed away, bowing low before it.

Seeing their prostration before his power, Harkhon smiled and raised his fiery hand high.

"You See now, Witch?" Harkhon said, snapping his hand shut into a fist, snuffing out the magical flame he'd created.

"I See only your death, Secondman," Sibyl said. "Nothing more."

Harkhon just laughed, a great, galloping guffaw.

"You're new to this place," he said. "Fresh-fleshed and green-souled. As I said, you haven't bathed in the magic of Soria. It will grow in you, as it does in every sensitive. You will grow stronger, as I have. You will taste the power, and find it as sweet as we all do. It was thus with the Manticore. I remember him, you know. I came here when he left this place, fully-formed, long ago. He fed on this jungle.

He drank in the magic, gorged upon it. And he grew powerful. Like Longmaw. Like Sansibarra. Like Dresdemina and Apharra. Like Rothgrim and Ephetris. Sorcererkings, all. One day, Harkhon of the Broken Road will join their exalted ranks. A sorcerer-king of Soria."

Sibyl listened to the magus, took in all that he had said. When he named the sorcerer-kings of Old Soria, she found that she could See them, for such was their power that the mere mention of their names conjured up their images in her mind. Sansibarra, a blue-white woman with matching hair, with only half a body, the rest long and serpentine, coiled around an ebony column. Ephetris, with the head of a jackal, a body made of brightest bronze, marking the passage of time with a great hourglass he carried with him, filled with sparkling light. Dresdemina, how like the Dragon she already was, but silver, not gold, and sinuous, sleeping in a massive temple of bluestone, in the depths of the neighboring Iron Jungle. Rothgrim howled in the heart of the Black Jungle, stalking the ruined streets of the long-dead capital city of Soria.

The ancient capital was once the center of the Empire, now the lair of monstrous, iron-clawed Rothgrim, whose roar could be heard across the Vale of Tears. Apharra, holding court beneath an endless night of her own imagining, her body like a sea of stars in the form of a woman, her all-seeing eyes never blinking, noticing Sibyl noticing her.

To even See them as she did was to make herself dizzy, for their power carried over in her sensing them, and Sibyl had to wipe more blood from her nose as it fell. Harkhon loved that, clapping his hands together in glee.

"You See! You See!" Harkhon said. "Witch, you See. The Manticore sloughed off his old name as readily as his

flesh. Who he was, he left upon the jungle floor like a cast-off skin, and became a god. A fate that awaits us all."

The magus grabbed Sibyl's hand.

"In time, you will appreciate and understand," Harkhon said. "I didn't believe. Before I came here, I didn't believe. But look at Longmaw. Behold him in his glory. No one knows how long he has haunted the Hollow Hall. Centuries? Millennia? Eons? Who is to say? Perhaps the Sorians fed Longmaw sacrifices even then, when their Empire was strong and held the world within its grasp. Can you See back that far?"

Sibyl jerked her hand free of the magus, making him pitch forward onto the white sand, face-first.

"I See only your death," Sibyl said. She yanked a dagger from the sand, stabbed Harkhon through his bare foot with it.

The magus howled and cursed, kicking at Sibyl with his unhurt foot.

"You stabbed me!" Harkhon cried, flailing out, reaching for one of the Wolf Knight's swords in the sand.

The Riverfolk looked on in wonder, their blank, powdered faces uncertain, for they had been conditioned to fear and obey the magus, who walked among them with arrogant impunity. It was not for them to interfere with his doings, and to see the wild-eyed woman in red attack him caused them great confusion.

Harkhon fought his way to his feet, brandishing the Dwarvish shortsword, his face full of rage. He called out in the well-rehearsed arcane language he knew by heart, and the shortsword burst into flame, prompting cries of wonder and terror among the Riverfolk.

Sibyl grabbed another of the swords, a cutlass with a bell-like brass hilt, and raised it to defend herself, while Harkhon held aloft the flaming blade, his kohl-smeared eyes upon her, wild and dark.

"*Factoremignis*," Sibyl said. "A parlor trick, magus. *Restinctusignis*."

Her words brought more blood to her nose and Harkhon's, and, for a moment, they contended beyond the space between them, and, to the dismay of the magus, the fire that danced upon the blade was snuffed out.

Harkhon's dark eyes widened at how easily she'd blocked him, before he lunged at her with the still-smoking blade. But his wounded and pinioned foot hobbled his attack, and he lurched forward, impaling himself on the cutlass that she wielded.

Sibyl stepped away from the fallen magician, who fought to regain his footing, crying out arcane words to try to restore himself, in the face of the damage done to him, while Sibyl spoke to him, out of reach, and the Riverfolk stepped back in a half-circle of wonder.

"You are undone," Sibyl said.

Harkhon pried the cutlass loose, braying words on bloodied lips, seeking to seal the mortal wound he'd received.

"I'm not ready," Harkhon said. "It's too soon."

Incredibly, the wound closed, and the blood flow ceased, and even Sibyl was impressed that this journeyman wizard could do such a thing.

Harkhon regained some of his confidence, as if even he could not believe his own good fortune.

"You See? The Black Jungle protects its own," Harkhon said. "You are strong, but I am stronger, still."

He tossed aside the cutlass, and bent to pry the dagger from his foot, yanking it out and casting it aside. He called out his incantations while rubbing his wounded foot with his trembling hands. Incredibly, the wound began to heal before her eyes.

Sibyl, whose nose bled forcefully at the unnatural bending of life and death woven by the magus, wiped the blood from her chin with the back of her hand, before laying her hands on the wizard's shoulders.

"Secondman," Sibyl, giving him a shove. "You shall be the first to fall."

Harkhon looked up at her, startled, as he stumbled backward on the ivory shore, falling into the blue-white water.

The Magus of the Broken Road cried out as he fell into the poison lake, splashing and vanishing from view with a gurgling shriek cut off by the inrushing water, while the Riverfolk began to murmur and wail, pointing and gesturing to Sibyl.

She stood there with bloodied hands and chin, daubing the blood from her nose and halting the bolder of them with the radiant blue of her eyes, and with a whisper of an incantation.

"*Nepropiusveniunt!* Your master is dead," Sibyl said, glancing at the rippling water, wondering if Harkhon would emerge. But there were only some stray, bluish bubbles, no sign of him. The Riverfolk fled from the Mandrian witch, running off into the jungle with cries of awe and wonder at the sudden and unthinkable demise of their master. Drops of blood from Sibyl flecked the white-sanded beach.

She stared at the island, where Farys scaled the white temple tower, pursued by Longmaw. Then she turned her gaze toward the tribal canoe, beached upon the shore.

Five

Farys scaled the white ziggurat, Longmaw close on his heels, bellowing for him, his great, webbed forelimbs finding ready purchase on the statues.

The great god-beast's mouth hung open as it climbed, looking like nothing so much as a tooth-filled fissure, its pink tongue at the ready.

It was gaining on him, and Farys waited for it to launch its tongue at him once more, the massive muscle flicking out toward him like a striking snake, smacking against the whitestone with a gooey slap.

Wasting no time, Farys lunged at the tongue, stabbing it with the spear, which pierced through the mass of flesh. The spear passed through it, going through one of the holes in the whitestone temple. It held fast, as Longmaw roared its pain and rage, unable to draw back its tongue, which was effectively locked in place by the amberwood spear.

Farys smiled to himself, slipping over the other side of the temple, while Longmaw scaled the tower, trying to free itself.

He reached the other side of the temple, searching for something he could use as a weapon, while Longmaw finally managed to yank its tongue free of the spear, its globular tongue splitting as it tore loose, the spear falling through the hole, landing in the half-lit interior of the temple. Longmaw's blood splashed against the stone and fell through the holes in the temple, raining down on the ground.

"A god who bleeds," Farys said.

The Wolf Knight grabbed some of the free stones, while Longmaw, enraged, dropped down from above, landing on the ground with a titanic thump. Its pearlescent skin was marred by its own blood, which stained its lips, which were bared to reveal its great blue-white teeth.

"Sorry," Farys said, smirking at it.

Longmaw charged Farys, who quickly put the tree between Longmaw and him. Longmaw's great, broad head struck the massive mujandi tree with a crunch, the wood of the tree bending, but not breaking.

Farys charged Longmaw, actually scaling up the front of the thing, sliding past its lethal mouth and slipping down its back, upon which was an almost sail-like fin.

Longmaw lashed its finned tail at Farys, catching the Wolf Knight and knocking him into the White Temple, where he slid down the stone ramp, yelling as he splashed into the waist-deep, bloodied water.

The god-monster bellowed, the sound echoing deafeningly in the sun-dappled tower, while Farys followed the blood trail in the water to reclaim his spear.

Longmaw's shadow filled the archway that led into the temple, blocking out the archway light, and Farys felt he could hear some satisfaction in the growl of the beast, as it slithered down the ramp, landing in the water with a massive splash that sent a surge of water at Farys, nearly knocking him over.

Farys felt more than a little fear in the water, as the great beast side-slithered smoothly toward him, sending another great wave in the temple water as it did so.

As outside, Farys used the columns to put a barrier between himself and the monster, bracing for the inevitable impact of its advance. Longmaw struck the column Farys hid behind, the stone holding fast.

Farys struck at Longmaw with his spear, the stone point piercing the pearly sheen of its head, drawing more blood. Longmaw opened its great mouth in growing rage at the elusive and troublesome meal.

Longmaw lurched again at Farys, who held his position behind the protection of the columns. Longmaw roared again, its ragged, forked tongue flicking out, trying to find purchase on the Wolf Knight, who again managed to dodge it, throwing the spear hard down the throat of Longmaw, who all but swallowed the spear, which lodged itself in its throat.

This terribly distracted the monster, which fought to free its throat of the painful barb. While it was trying to cough out the spear, Farys waded past the creature, heading for the slippery ramp, moving past it, heading for the honeycombed walls, through which the light of the day flowed like hope.

Farys leaped for the side wall of the temple, climbing hand over hand, heading toward the archway, while Longmaw coughed out the amberwood spear, turning itself around to continue its pursuit of the Wolf Knight.

It slithered in the water, half-leaping to try to snap at Farys, who lifted his legs out of its reach. His eyes stole to the shore of the island, where Sibyl had arrived by way of a canoe.

She ran to the entrance of the temple, gazing in bloody-eyed disgust at the monstrosity splashing in the water.

"A little help, perchance?" Farys asked.

"Indeed," Sibyl said, throwing the Dwarvish shortsword up to Farys, who caught it with an outstretched hand.

"Ah, Stillicha," Farys said. "A bit smaller than I should like, but I can hardly complain."

"Longmaw," Sibyl said, her voice ringing out in the confines of the temple. "*Osmeumescaptivus.*"

The crackle of magic shook the stones of the temple, striking Longmaw, who shook off her attack as if it hadn't happened. The great god-beast seemed to cackle, charging up the ramp, heading for Sibyl with mouth agape.

As it passed beneath him, intent on taking the witch, Farys dropped from where he had been hanging, piercing Longmaw's great, wide carapace with the Dwarvish blade, which peeled its white-hued flesh easily. The Wolf Knight used the sword as a grapnel, climbing his way up Longmaw and out of the temple, tumbling past its flailing jaws, reaching the blinding sand.

The two of them ran for the canoe, while the wounded Longmaw slithered bloodily from the archway of the white temple.

Farys managed to get on the canoe first, steadying it, while Sibyl ran to the canoe, Longmaw stagger-galloping toward the shore, close behind, splashing its own island shore with its blood.

Farys took her arm in his, pulling her aboard, and grabbing one of the oars and rowing as quickly as he could, while Longmaw stormed and bellowed.

They moved out of reach of the beast, which pawed at the ground with its massive webbed talons.

"It used to be a man," Sibyl said, wiping her nose and gazing at the bleeding beast. "Long ago."

"What happened to him?" Farys asked.

"This place did," Sibyl said, gazing around them with concern upon her face. "We are in the heart of Soria, Farys. Their poison courses through this land, just as I said before."

"Dark magic here, yes," Farys said, but the Mandrian turned her gaze upon him, her blue eyes bloodshot.

"No," Sibyl said. "Far, far more than that."

"What happened to Harkhon?" Farys asked.

"I took him for a swim in his poison lake," Sibyl said, glancing in the toxic water around them. Farys laughed.

As they rowed, Longmaw stormed before its lonely temple, and Sibyl raised her hands overhead. And the skies over the Black Jungle cracked and broke open, bathing the knight and witch alike in cleansing rain that splashed in the blue-white of the deadly lake.

It felt close enough to freedom in this hellish place.

Farys rowed them ashore, by the forest of his swords, keen to rescue them from the driving rain, while horse-meat burned and sizzled in the fires that were fast quenching in the deluge.

"Did you bring the storm?" Farys asked of the witch, who gazed back at the Temple of Longmaw, the god-monster of the lonely island, and at the stormy sky above. Her eyes were now orbs of bright blue upon a sea of red.

"I did," Sibyl said. "You should not have brought me here, Farys."

✦ ✦ ✦

Six

farys recovered his swords, putting them in their scabbards, with Tempest at his side once more, bringing him a measure of comfort, while he and Sibyl went to one of the huts of the Riverfolk, having taking some of the horsemeat to eat before the fading fires further claimed it.

The Wolf Knight was angry at the loss of their mounts, was determined not to let them go to waste, but his concern was more on Sibyl, who looked as if she had fallen ill.

She had stretched out on a great mujandi leaf that served as a makeshift bed upon the white sand within the thatched hut.

"Your eyes," Farys said. "They're blood red."

"I know," Sibyl said. "The magic of this place is…potent."

"Perhaps we can find something to treat you in Arokhnai," Farys said, offering her some of the horsemeat. Sibyl refused it, curled in a ball upon the mujandi leaf. "It's going to take rather longer to reach it than before. And lord knows the Riverfolk will make it a challenging trek."

"You are always so flippant," Sibyl said. "You cannot even feel it, can you?"

Farys sighed. "I'm a Borderlander. I'm not a magician. I'm insensitive to such things. Not to your plight, mind you, but to magic, itself. I know it exists, but I can't waste time worrying about it."

Sibyl scoffed. "How lucky for you. You see a path, you take the path. I see the paths upon the paths, and the divergences and cosmic confluences. Every path I take is a crux, an apex, and a nexus."

Farys ate while the thunder boomed, and Longmaw raged in the driving rain, still visible in the distance, a white bulk upon his island.

"I was counting on your ability to See," Farys said. "I need that."

"The Manticore marinated in this place," Sibyl said. "Not here. Not Lake Harkhon. Elsewhere."

"You named it after the magus?" Farys said. "That seems almost cruel."

"Yes," Sibyl said. "A name as good as any. The fool wanted power and immortality. Let him be the spirit of the poisoned lake. I have bound him to it."

"What?" Farys asked, pausing in his feasting.

"I bound him to the lake," Sibyl said. "I threw him into the water, where he died from it, the poison of the water consumed him. His shade raged at me from the depths, for what I had done, how I had ruined him. So, I bound him to the lake."

"What does that mean?" Farys asked.

Sibyl sneered, touching her face with her hands, while her red-hued eyes of blue stared out at the shambling Longmaw.

"It means that his spirit will forever haunt this place," Sibyl said. "It will be his home and his prison, that he might dwell upon the error of his ways, at having confronted us, trying to sacrifice you to that monster and to

tempt me to become like him. He sought power, so let him have it in the dreadful lake, forevermore."

"You can do that?"

"It's called a curse, Farys," Sibyl said. "I simply cursed him. A child could do such things. But in this place, even childish things are magnified—a child might as well be a titan. I See why they come, the hermit wizards. The magi. The Manticore. I See it."

Farys resumed eating, leaning in, intently.

"What do you See?" Farys asked.

"Everything," Sibyl said. "The Manticore is like Valtara, the Fire Sphinx of the Iron Jungle."

"Who?" Farys asked. "The Iron Jungle is west of here."

"Never mind," Sibyl said. "You'll learn about her soon enough."

"Wait, what are you saying?" Farys asked.

"The future, Farys," Sibyl said. "I have Seen it. I've Seen her. She is more splendid than the Manticore by far. How easy it would be."

Farys stopped eating again, wrapping the remaining meat in stray mujandi leaves, and reached out for the witch, touching her forehead.

"You're feverish," Farys said.

"I'm not," Sibyl said. "We make our way to Mercanto. Not yet. Many miles to cross."

"Mercanto," Farys said. "Yes, I have a friend, there. Arkhan."

"He is Emperor Arkhan, now," Sibyl said. "Of Mercanto, for the past five years. But not for long, alas. Valtara flies forth to depose him, for reasons only she knows. His days in power are numbered."

She counted them off on her fingers, silently—five, four, three, two, one.

"Emperor," Farys said. "I can't see him as an emperor. Fiss'Q would be amused."

"Fiss'Q," Sibyl said. "We're seeing her soon."

It wasn't a question, and Farys looked at the witch with a measure of concern.

"Yes," Farys said. "At Arokhnai. But you were talking about the Manticore before."

"Like a caterpillar," Sibyl said. "Bound up, then bursting free of his old skin. This place. It offers godhead to those who might dare take it. The ruins of this empire are filled with little temples, with little gods, demigods, godlings."

"Godlings?" Farys asked.

"Like Longmaw," Sibyl said.

"Why would a man wish to become such a thing?" Farys asked, glancing out at the white beast, which roared blindly in the driving rain.

"We are creatures of our appetites," Sibyl said. "For Longmaw, perhaps the appetite was all that remained. Even now, he heals from the wounds you gave him. He will be whole again soon, though worry not—the lake contains him. He cannot swim after us."

"That's certainly some good news," Farys said."

He bound up his swords with a leather strap.

"I'm going to leave the rest of it here, I think," Farys said. "Not the gold, of course. But my armor. I'm only taking the swords. And my shield."

Sibyl smiled, blood tears at her eyes, traveling down her cheeks. Seeing them, Farys gestured, as if to warn her.

"I know," Sibyl said. "You have no idea what I know, now."

Seven

They slept in the hut, while the monsoon raged, and Sibyl tossed and turned in feverish sleep. Her blood-soaked gaze let her See far beyond the here and now, to the there and then, and the never and forever.

It could have been said that she was dreaming, but she knew it to be no dream—she was, rather, the prism of probability, luck's lens, and saw the paths of possibility radiating out. To See, and to See through, this was her blessed curse.

She Saw hapless Harkhon of the Broken Road, his bound shade shrieking in the milky blue waters of his namesake lake, and dread Longmaw, imprisoned on his temple island, enraged at the emptiness of his stomach, owed a sacrifice he did not require, but merely desired, and was denied.

And Longmaw saw her Seeing him, and, for a moment, his rage was quieted, and they beheld one another, witch and monstrosity. It was as if they were kin, and she could See the soul at the heart of the monster. She could see who he had been before, the Secondman of Valdikan, the magus, Longinus, his broad grin and carefully drawn maps of the Black Jungle, the lore of the land. Centuries ago, a hopeful journey.

"This is what you have become," Sibyl said.

"I am as I have made me," Longmaw answered, without his lips moving, his thoughts like the pounding of the drums of his worshippers.

And then, Longmaw attacked her with his mind, sending a wave of force that flew out from him like a great wave, blasting Sibyl away in a burst of pain and torment. Debased he was, but Longmaw was powerful. Farys had been fortunate to have lived as long as he had in his battle with the god-beast, standing as he did upon a mountain of sacrifices and the worship of the Rivermen.

Centuries of worship by the Riverfolk, each sacrifice taken to the island and fed to Longmaw. Strangers, rival tribes. Anyone they could fetch for him, his endless appetite. The poison pool of the lake, his own creation? He could no longer remember, but it ensured that no one came to his island temple recklessly.

How the days and years blended, until the wizard Longinus was only the barest of memories, and the god-monster Longmaw now supplanted him. The other things, the other desires, they faded away as his appetite for knowledge turned into something more primal, and he saw himself change in stages, to progress, but only to a point, and to pass no further beyond that point. Not a god. That would be denied him. More than just a monster, and less than a true god, like the others. Something in between.

The reverence of the Riverfolk bound him to that place. Their fear and awe fed him as surely as the sacrifices did, and he craved it, drew strength from it. Lines between

them and him, something only someone like Sibyl could See.

"*Egointellegote,*" Sibyl said.

"*Pythonissam,*" Longmaw said, sending another wave of force at her, stronger than before. Sibyl found herself hurled Irthward by the power of Longmaw's mind, itself a thunderbolt far greater than the storm that raged in the sky over them, and she fell into a deep sleep.

Eight

Sibyl did not quite wake up from the Blood Fever that claimed her. Rather, she'd sat up with a gasp, blood flowing down her cheeks from her eyes, and the gestured, and, as suddenly as it had begun, the storm ceased, as if the crack in the sky had been sealed shut.

Then she fell back upon the mujandi, and could not be awakened, despite the efforts of Farys.

"Sibyl, Sibyl," Farys said. "You're a mess. You need to wake up."

But she was insensate, and Farys cursed, glancing outside, seeing the mists rising from the jungle around them, the great heat rolling back in even now, as soon as the storm had ceased. Somewhere, he could hear the cries of the Riverfolk, who would return at some point.

Farys put his hand upon her chest, and felt a heartbeat. The heat that flowed off of her was great. He was no metaphysician, but she looked feverish. He thought it imperative that they get to Arokhnai sooner than later.

"Sorry to have brought you to this place," Farys said. "I had no idea what it would do to you."

He peered out of the hut, and spied the canoe upon the shore. Beyond it, on the island, Longmaw had finally retreated back to its white temple, and the jungle, for the moment, was uncannily still.

Farys ran to the canoe, which was filled with rainwater from the storm. He drank his fill from the water, and soaked some rags with it, before overturning it to dump out the rest, and dragged it across the ivory sand to the thatched hut.

Then he went to the jungle's edge, hacking some vines with Tempest, cutting this way and that, and brought them back as well.

He picked up some mujandi leaves and lined the canoe with them, and then hefted Sibyl, gently setting her into it, along with their gear that had been taken from the horses. He used one of the wet rags to mop the blood from Sibyl's face, then placed another on her forehead, to help keep her cool.

"I changed my mind about abandoning the horses' things. Can't leave them for the bloody Rivermen," Farys said. "They don't deserve them, after what they've put us through."

Then he wound the vines through the canoe, until he turned it into a kind of sledge. He then proceeded to drag it away from Lake Harkhon, taking advantage of the soaked ground to make the passage of the makeshift travois somewhat easier.

The Riverfolk were watching the Wolf Knight go from the shadows of the trees and vines, their green faces registering mute disapproval, the white paint they'd worn having run down their skin in streaks that made them appear striped.

Their hard eyes took in the canoe that bore the witch who had slain their magus-master, and they called out

to each other with bird songs, gripping spears and bows, trailing after Farys, fearful of approaching, but stalking him, all the same. He hoped they'd not launch their poison arrows as him. With Sibyl downed, he'd not last long against that sort of attack.

Farys reached the Broken Road again, having drawn Tempest, letting the green-hued blade be seen by the Riverfolk, who spread out, muttering to each other in angry tones.

The canoe scraped along the broken stone of the road to Arokhnai, leaving a path that anyone could follow.

Farys felt his heart pound as he transported Sibyl this way. If they could only make it to the river that led to Arokhnai—the big, beautiful Jade River—it would be an easier thing. But, by his estimation, they were three days from Arokhnai by horse, so a week out by foot. And the Jade River would not reveal itself for at least a day by foot. Maybe longer at the rate he was going.

The bolder of the Riverfolk emerged from the shelter of the jungle to call out to Farys in anger.

Farys paused in his travel to turn and confront them.

"You can have your canoe back when I'm through with it," Farys said. "I'm only borrowing it, I swear to you."

One of the Rivermen—perhaps the chieftain—lobbed a spear at Farys, the spear impaling the ground only inches from Farys. The Chieftain, as Farys viewed him, beat his chest with his hand, defiant, and pointed to Sibyl.

"Mofasi," the Chieftain said.

"No," Farys said. "You can't have her."

Although the green-skinned Riverfolk could not understand his words, they clearly got his intent, and angrily

47

remonstrated him with hoots and hollers, waving their spears and bows in the air.

"You. Can't. Have. Her." Farys said, snatching up the Chieftain's spear and hurling it back at him, catching him in the chest with it. The Chieftain gasped, falling backward, dead, as the poison-tipped spear snuffed out his life in a heartbeat.

At the sight of their fallen leader, the Riverfolk charged Farys with hisses and hollers, who met them with Tempest and Stillicha, fighting in a sure-footed circle around Sibyl. He'd never fought these Riverfolk before, and though they had the numbers on him, and had their poison-coated spears and arrows, Farys was a far better-trained warrior than they were.

What's more, their wood-and-obsidian swords were no match for either Tempest or Stillicha, and the ground was soon littered with bits of broken wood and glass, and with the bodies of fallen Rivermen. Some of their sharp blades had cut him on his arms and legs, and he was bloodied, but was alive, and still able to fight.

Farys beat them back, and they gave him a wide berth, and he pointed at the canoe with the bloody short sword.

"She's with me," Farys said. "You cannot have her."

The Riverfolk were still unsatisfied with that answer, but with a half-dozen of their strongest warriors dead upon the Broken Road, were willing—for now—to concede the point.

Warily, Farys backed away from the carnage, and jabbed Stillicha into the wood of the canoe, and, holding Tempest in his hand, still, wore the vine like a garland, and began cautiously dragging Sibyl back down the Broken

Road, leaving the Riverfolk with their dead, and a trail of
his own blood in his wake.

Nine

Farys reached the Jade River in a bit over a day, with the angry-fearful Riverfolk of Lake Harkhon always dogging his steps. They did not engage after he'd killed their best warriors, but they also did not abandon their pursuit.

And yet, the Harkhonites—as Farys came to think of this tribe—would not flee. Nor would they let him sleep. At night, they would sing and dance in the dark, playing little drums and caterwauling, out of reach, but audible.

On that trek to the river, Sibyl herself wouldn't do anything except sleep. She murmured and tossed and turned, sweating and shaking. But she would not awaken, no matter what he did.

Farys gathered fresh water from some waxy, bowl-shaped leaves, and gave her some to drink, but Sibyl would still not fully awaken, even when her blood-soaked eyes would open and she would see things that he could not.

When the Harkhonites saw that Farys was nearing the Jade River, they became more aggressive, getting closer, launching poison arrows at Farys, while fleeing out of reach when he might deign to pursue them. This advance-retreat stalemate continued, as Farys painfully edged ever closer to the river.

Exhausted to the point of collapsing, Farys saw the Broken Road split in two by the width of the Jade River, and felt a measure of relief. While he could not simply rest upon the river, he at least could get ahead of the Harkhonites.

"Bloody jackals," Farys said, glowering at them. "Harkhon would be happy to know that I've named you after him. You live up to his name, bedeviling me as you do."

They watched him with their blank faces, having replaced their white body paint during the night, giving them frightening countenances, almost like ghosts. They were a blend of young men and women, and they called Farys a name, like it was an accusation.

"Kelaninna," they would call him. It was not a word that he knew, but they would say it, like a chant.

They would point to Sibyl and say "Kelaninna mofasi."

Sibyl stirred in the canoe, while Farys paused in his hauling the canoe, grabbing his shield from off his back, and charged at the Harkhonites, who scampered away, launching arrows at him, which struck his shield.

Frustrated, Farys let out a war cry, which was answered by the hooting Harkhonites, who would only close with Farys as he retreated. He carefully backpedaled toward Sibyl, his eyes on the Riverfolk, who were surging forward, step-by-step.

There were at least thirty of them, and Farys knew that he could not take more than half of them, at best, before they overtook him.

"Come on, then," Farys said, drawing a line against one of the cracked pavestones of the Broken Road with Tempest, the green blade easily scratching its mark with sparks upon the Sorian stone.

The Harkhonites sensed the challenge the Wolf Knight offered, and launched arrows at him again, which he blocked with his shield, the arrows landing with a rhythmic patter against the shield's face.

"I didn't think my last stand would be upon a godforsaken road in the midst of a cursed jungle," Farys said aloud, half to himself, half to the goddess, Fornia, known as Lady Luck.

Harkhonites howled and charged him, having switched from bows to spears, now, and Farys braced to receive their charge, come what may.

All at once, the air around them blurred, and Farys felt his skin tingle, felt his stomach clench, as he heard Sibyl murmur behind him.

"*Factisuntarbores!*" Sibyl chanted. "*Factisuntarbores! Factisuntarbores!*"

He dared to steal a glance, and saw her upright in the canoe, arms out in front of her, clawing the air with her hands, a bloody snarl upon her face. She gazed out with her bleeding eyes, bright blue orbs against the sea of blood around them, bloody lines running down her cheeks.

And when Farys turned his attention back to the Harkhonites, he was amazed to see, where there had been thirty Riverfolk, there were, now, thirty young mujandi trees, wound in tangled patterns, as if struck by a storm, their bark smeared with white paint, with strands of beads dangling from their branches.

He could divine the shapes of the Harkhonites in the trees, and saw the handful of Riverfolk who had hung back now running away, jabbering to themselves in terror as they went, until they vanished from view.

"Sibyl," Farys said. "What have you done?"

"Saved you," Sibyl said, laughing to herself, a dry, rasping thing. "Yet again."

Farys stepped back to the canoe, sighing, helping her out of it. She wiped her bloody face with the back of her hand.

"Are you recovered from the Blood Fever?" Farys asked. "It was a near thing for awhile, there."

"It is not Blood Fever," Sibyl said. "And, no, I am not recovered. Blood magic fever, more like."

"You turned those Harkhonites into mujandi trees," Farys said.

Sibyl conjured up a goblet, out of thin air, and drank from it, as if it was the most normal thing in the world. There was some sort of amber-colored wine in the golden goblet. Farys watched this with amazement and more than a little concern.

"I was planning to take us down the river, toward Arokhnai," Farys said. "If that is amenable to you. I think we should get you out of this jungle, Sibyl."

"Yes," Sibyl said. "While you still can. While I still can."

She downed the conjured cup of wine and tossed the goblet aside, the thing landing on the broken pavestones with a clang as it rolled away.

Farys pointed out the approach he planned to take, sliding the canoe off the Broken Road, and through a slippery path that led to the winding Jade River, while Sibyl followed him.

"I saw things while I slept," Sibyl said. "Many, many things."

The Wolf Knight edged the canoe into the water, holding out his hand for Sibyl, who took it, slipping herself aboard. Steadying the canoe, Farys boarded and took up the oar, shoving off, sending them downstream.

"Tell me what you saw," Farys said.

"In time," Sibyl said.

"Now would be a good time," Farys said.

"Later would be better," Sibyl said, meeting his eyes with her own bloodstained gaze.

Ten

The Jade River wound like a great jungle snake, and grew ever broader as they made their way down it, clearing the jungle canopy, and moving into massive marshland, where the river grasses grew twice as tall as Farys, and swayed and hummed with the sound of insects and birds.

A dozen jungle crows had gotten wind of Sibyl, and had begun to follow them, cawing and flitting about from tree to tree. They were bigger than the crows that usually accompanied her, with great, broad bills that made them look almost like ravens.

"You've made some friends, it would seem," Farys said.

"Yes," Sibyl said. "They'll protect us. What happened after the hut?"

"You stopped the storm," Farys said. "And I made good our escape from Longmaw and the lake. But the Harkhonites didn't make it easy. I fear we did great harm to their tribe. It'll be a story they'll not soon forget. I imagine they'll be telling the story of Greensword and the Bloody-Eyed Witch for generations around their campfires."

"Debased humans," Sibyl said. "Halfmen, tainted by Sorian magic. Another millennium, they'll be even more reptilian than they already are. You can't escape it. The motes are everywhere."

"Motes?" Farys asked.

"It's hard to explain in a manner you would understand," Sibyl said.

Farys smirked at her. "Try me, but do please use small words, and talk slowly."

"Sorian magic is borne upon tiny motes. Like dust. We travel through a sea of them in the Black Jungle. We breathe them in. Even you."

"Even me," Farys said.

"It's like the ghost of the Sorians. Their power in their day must have been unimaginable," Sibyl said. "All that remains of them, now. But still potent. Still dangerous."

"I see," Farys said.

"If only you could," Sibyl said. "Then your eyes would bleed for what you had seen."

"How can something I can't see affect me?" Farys said. Sibyl managed a smile, and, on her strong features, it was a pleasant smile, despite their circumstances.

"There are so many things you can't see that can affect you," Sibyl said. "All around us, the motes fly. I have Seen it."

"At any rate," Farys said. "I hauled you through the jungle, with the Harkhonites haunting my every step. You were no help at all, I'm afraid. Until that last bit at the end."

Out of the protective cover of the Black Jungle, there was only the unforgiving heat of the relentless sun beating down upon them, and both of them made makeshift hats out of mujandi leaves to protect themselves. They laughed at each other, with their big, broadleafed mujandi hats.

"Fiss'Q will have a good laugh at us over this," Farys said. "Quite the statement we're making with these."

"I like them," Sibyl said. "My people don't tend to wear hats, but I enjoy them. Especially in this awful Southland sun."

"Some of the women of Arokhnai make great hats with holes in their crowns," Farys said. "And they sit on the roofs of their townhomes, letting the sun bleach their hair, while they are protected in the shade."

Sibyl grimaced at the thought.

"That sounds horrible," she said, touching her own golden hair.

"They do it, all the same," Farys said.

Sibyl had pried Stillicha out of the wood of the canoe, toying with it, letting the short blade catch the bright sunlight. The auri was such a beautiful metal, and the workmanship was exemplary.

"What does 'Stillicha' mean?" Sibyl asked. "I don't speak Dwarvish. Wait, I know these words. 'Stickler.' That's what it means, yes?"

"Yes," Farys said. "Dwarvish humor."

He couldn't help but wonder about her condition, if that was even the word for it. Farys paddled them carefully down the river, exhausted eyes still alert for danger. He entertained visions of sleeping safely in Arokhnai. The prospect of rest was intoxicating.

Sibyl noticed that Farys had bandaged his arms, and the blood that had stained his tunic.

"You're hurt," Sibyl said.

"Just a little," Farys said. She gazed at him with the Sight, and Farys could feel his skin crawl from the force of her gaze.

"The Riverfolk cut you with their obsidian blades," Sibyl said. "You fought them off."

"I did, indeed," Farys said.

"Such sharp stones," Sibyl said. "Volcanic glass."

"What?" Farys asked.

"The obsidian," Sibyl said. "The weapons of the Riverfolk."

"Ah," Farys said. Sibyl clutched her arms around herself, as if a chill passed through her, despite the ungodly heat of the day.

"I think the Manticore used the magic of that dreadful jungle to grow powerful," Sibyl said. "He is like Longmaw, and the Dragon. Only differing in degree. I could follow that path. I could, perhaps, be as powerful as the Dragon, if I wanted to. If I stayed here, I could saturate myself with the motes and grow ever more powerful."

She looked at Farys from beneath the shadow of the mujandi leaf, her bloody eyes staring hard at him.

"I could be the Mofasi of those Harkhonites," Sibyl said. "They would worship me, and I could grow even more terribly powerful. I could hunt down the god-emperors of the jungles and kill them all, drawing forth their power into me. And then I would hunt down the Dragon. The Dragon fears this."

Farys chose his next words carefully, fearful of where they might take him.

"But you won't do that," Farys said.

Sibyl trailed her bloody hands in the water a moment, rinsing them clean.

"Not yet," Sibyl said. "I would not want to end up like Him. I fear that I would more than lose my way out here. I would lose myself, as well. As surely as Longinus became Longmaw, so I would cease to be Sibyl of Mandria, and would become something else. Something monstrous."

"What is a 'Mofasi,' anyway?" Farys said. "I heard them say those words."

"It is a 'Ghost-Goddess' to the Harkhonites," Sibyl said.

"I don't think you should become a Ghost Goddess," Farys said. "What's a 'Kelannina,' then?"

Sibyl smiled to herself a moment, a ghoulish look in her current state, but the smile was radiant, all the same, the blood on her face like warpaint.

"It is a 'Protector,'" Sibyl said.

Eleven

The White Towers of Arokhnai seemed to rise up out of the Sorian Sea, buttressed by the marshlands and mangroves that increasingly became salt marshes, to the point of sharks being visible in the turbid water of the Jade River. Their fins flanked them a few times, only to swim away.

The Towers were whitestone, reminiscent of Longmaw's own temple, and seeing them made Farys uneasy. The Great Clock Tower of Arokhnai could also be seen, safely ensconced between the minarets. A wonder of Irth, the Clock Tower, a blackstone rectangular spire with a pointed roof and a great circular face upon it, broke time up into segments, and tolled out the time every so often with a gong that could be heard from a great distance. Farys didn't understand the purpose of the Great Clock Tower, but for those in Arokhnai, the timely tolling of its bells were significant to the citizen of the city.

"Arokhnai is a mercantile city," Farys said. "To my knowledge, time is almost more precious than gold to them."

"You don't need to tell me about it," Sibyl said. "I know. The pearl of the Slaver Cities, rich, ancient, and powerful. Seeking to climb out from under the yoke of this infernal historic association, they have long since banned slave-trading in their city to become a free republic, to the scorn and derision of the other Slaver Cities. Their merchant princes sail around the world, making trade and bringing wealth back home, including copious trade in spices, drugs, poisons, and exotic fragrances. Arokhnai is tripartite-ruled. It is ruled by a Commission of sea captains, with a trade Guild forming the second center of power. The third, and most powerful, branch is that of the Shadowlanders themselves, who are the least in number, and call themselves the House of Shadows, also known as the Shadow Senate. The Commission, the Guild, and the Senate rule Arokhnai. Your friend, Fiss'Q, is a Senator. They are among the elite of Arokhnai, and protect it from the wrath of rivals by virtue of their skill at battle, assassination, and intrigue. Their Clock Tower attempts to carve up time into tidy intervals, and serves as a daily reminder to the people of Arokhnai that their time is fleeting in this world."

Farys looked at Sibyl a moment, concern etched upon his brow, for she had the right of it, down to every detail.

"Yeah, it's, uh, that," Farys said. "It's like you've been there, already."

"I have," Sibyl said. "I have Seen this place in my fever dreams. The Manticore was here, two centuries ago. He landed at his place, before he traveled into the jungle. It could be said that the Manticore was born in Arokhnai."

Farys wondered how she could See all of that.

"And who birthed him?" Farys asked, drowsing in the stern of the canoe, while the Towers of Arokhnai rose ever higher, onion-shaped and miraculous.

"A Shadowlander," Sibyl said. "A Shadow Warrior named Valonnis. A rival of Q'rr'k's, the Shadow Lord of Arokhnai."

Farys knew of Q'rr'k only because of Fiss'Q. He had been her master, long ago. He remembered her telling him of Q'rr'k, when the two of them lounged above the vice dens of Forlarin, the City of Emptied Souls, on the Obsidian Island.

Fiss'Q had stood in her lean-limbed, ebony splendor, her long black hair tied back with a golden knotted braid. With regal features and dark red eyes, her perfect form made her appear more sculpted than born.

She was a warrior like himself, but a Southland warrior, a different creature who fought different wars in different ways. What's more, she was a Shadowlander, which made her something altogether greater—and, in a way, less—than the wandering knight he had become.

Honor was terribly important to her, but Southland honor was very different from Northland honor. What would have been the genesis of a Northland blood feud was more a passing difference of opinion in the South-lands.

"How do you like the harouna, Farys?" Fiss'Q asked, while Farys puffed on the fragrant vapors from the stem of the brass pipe she had handed him.

"Magical," Farys said, flexing his sword hand in front of his eyes, moving his fingers this way and that. He saw everything that his sword hand was and would ever be, in that moment. He saw victory and defeat in the flex of his fingers.

"Only the Seeming," said Fiss'Q. "Harouna merely mas-querades as magical, Secondman. Streetside charlatans ped-

dle it in Forlarin, makeshift mystics serve it up in spiritual salons upon the Streets of Seeming."

He only half-remembered the story she had told him, and, because of the influence of the harouna, felt that he had actually been there.

"Let me show you some other things you might consider magical, my dear," Fiss'Q said, sliding close to him, her red eyes filling his vision.

"Farys," Sibyl said, awakening him from his reverie. "We are at Arokhnai."

Twelve

They reached the guarded harbor of Arokhnai feeling faintly ridiculous in their Harkhonite canoe, wearing their mujandi leaf sunhats, but if any were inclined to mock them, the mockery withered in their throats when they gazed upon Sybil's blood-red eyes and saw the clutch of swords Farys carried over his shoulder, and the blood that stained his tunic. Farys bribed the harbormaster to allow them a berth, and suggested that he could keep the canoe if he liked.

They paid a porter to load the cargo of their canoe upon a two-wheeled cart drawn by a pair of runners, while they tossed their mujandi leaf hats into the harbor, a kind of sacrifice to the Jade River.

As it was surrounded by marshes, Arokhnai had a low wall around her as protection, and the city depended heavily on her navy to protect her from attackers, as well. The harbor had been hewn from the banks of the river, and was screened from the open sea by part of the city.

Arokhnai straddled the wide mouth of the Jade River, leaving an opulent, smaller North Bank, and an industrious South Bank, where the majority of the city resided. These two parts of the city were connected by great stonework bridges that were themselves marvelous feats of Sorian engineering.

Farys had given the runners the address for Fiss'Q, or where he'd last known her to live, and the two of them ate heartily from the harbor vendors, who offered fried fish and shiny blue garria fruit, freshly harvested and shipped in from the plentiful plantations of Ankora. They ate and drank eagerly as the runners navigated them past the busy wharves and quays, as they made their way into Arokhnai proper.

The whitestone towers loomed like seven sentinels, and Farys held his tongue, for he was both exhausted and ravenous, and assumed that Sibyl, in her current state, already knew everything to know about Arokhnai that there was to know, anyway.

He gave her sidelong glances, noting that her blood-red eyes seemed perhaps a somewhat lighter shade, more of a pinkish hue, with fewer blood tears. She noticed him observing her.

"What?" Sibyl asked.

"How are you feeling?" Farys asked, between bites of garria fruit.

"Grateful," Sibyl said. "The air is cleaner, here."

Farys nodded. "The sea air always helps."

They passed within the walls of Arokhnai, and into the crowded streets, within the shadow of the towers.

The noise and traffic of the main street of Arokhnai was significant, with vendors at their stalls, protected by an overhanging tarp that would take the rain as it fell and channel it to special cisterns. Streets were lined with fragrant trees, which provided spots of shade and lent a pleasant atmosphere to the city.

The cart runners were, despite the milling crowds of tradesmen, able to navigate smoothly through Arokhnai. The scent of the spices was itself intoxicating, communicating exotic locations and dangerous destinations.

"Anything can be had here," Farys said, almost absently, as if he were lost in thought.

"I see," Sibyl said. "This is an ancient city. The Sorians would auction slaves here, while masked Southlanders kept their books."

"There are Southland merchant clans, here," Farys said. "They're part of the Guilds. We're not likely to have to deal with them, or to want to, unless we are looking to negotiate contracts with them."

Sibyl nodded. "I should like to see them. I heard stories of them as a girl, the strange servants of Soria."

"I was tutored by one as a boy," Farys said, and Sibyl could See his sorrow, though he tried to hide it. She wanted to console him, but didn't want to embarrass him. The pain he carried with him was deep inside, and he would resent her Seeing it at all.

"I would enjoy meeting one," Sibyl said. "So strange, to wear masks the way they do."

"After we've found Fiss'Q," Farys said. "There'll be time. Frankly, once I meet up with Fiss'Q, I only want to rest. Your adoring Harkhonites were nearly the death of me, Mofasi."

Sibyl could see the fatigue and pain behind the Wolf Knight's words, and wanted to comfort him, but for her own shame at being so afflicted by the Black Jungle. She had not known what to expect in that place, but the temptation to run off into the jungle and become a ghost-goddess remained a powerful one that stirred within her.

It had been as plain as day, that fervid fate. She Saw herself in the depths of the jungle, with a lost temple of her own, the surviving Harkhonites singing songs of praise, while she drank in the motes and grew powerful. She would meet the Knights of Mandria upon the shores of Lake Harkhon and slay them, having their golden helmets mounted on the ends of their golden lances, impaling their severed heads.

She would have raised their headless bodies from the dead and marched them back to Mandria, having their voices speak as they rode forth in a dreadful procession.

"We Knights of Mandria have fallen before the great Mofasi, the Dragonslayer," they would say, terrifying the Mandrians to see those severed heads at the point of their golden lances, speaking their doleful words.

The Dragon, in His infernal rage, would then send His armies into the Black Jungle, where Sibyl, the Ghost-Goddess of the bleeding eyes, would destroy them. She could See this great war, the Mandrian War, and take comfort in it.

For in that war, the Mandrians would fall before her endless Sight, into trap after trap she'd set for them, and the savage tribes of Old Soria would unite under her bloodied gaze. And she would corral the surviving petty gods and godlings of Old Soria and send them north into Mandria, where the surviving legions of the Dragon would recoil in horror at the manifold monstrosities that mauled their countryside. Sibyl smiled at the thought of Longmaw, now chained to her as a terrifying pet, stuffing himself on Mandrian knights.

The revenge would be sweet, and the burning of the capital city, Orelia, would be sweeter, still. The devastation

would be glorious, and the ruination of the Dragon, absolute. She would appear before Him when She was ready, and slay the god. She would melt Him down into coins She would distribute throughout the Kingdom in a grand gesture of cruelest charity. She would kill King Orelian, and all of the Royal Family, and hang their corpses from the walls of the capital in gilded gibbets. Sibyl would be the final end of Mandria.

And, when the Dragon was fallen, the gold that He had been all given away, She would rise up in His place, Her own origins lost to any but Herself. Mofasi, the Ghost-Goddess of Old Soria, Bringer of Ruin and Slayer of Dragons.

The Mandrians would pray to Her, as they had prayed to Him, in hopes of gaining a fraction of Her power through supplication. Her most ardent followers would create a great whitestone statue of Sibyl, from which blood tears would flow into a great reflecting pool. She would see young Mandrian women, Her priestesses, drinking from the blood tears from Her own idol, in hopes of gaining Her power of prophecy and true sight.

And it would begin all over again.

The Mofasi would become the new blight of Irth, the source of terror and tyranny. Seeing all, Seeing through all. Her priestesses would paint their faces white with streaks of red paint down their cheeks to mimic Her own bleeding eyes, and they would dance beneath the light of the sun and the moon in fearful processions, seeking out Her enemies. The enemies of Mofasi would be sacrificed to Her, of course, in a manner that pleased the Ghost-Goddess.

Sibyl dragged herself away from that fateful vision with a gasp, as the cart stopped at the address Farys had given the runners. It was a lovely townhome, a whitewashed portico before a heavy blackwood door, upon which had been carved polished images of fruit-bearing trees, made menacing by the glossy black of the wood, providing a stark contrast with the white that surrounded it.

Farys paid the cart runners, and rapped on the door, which had a great brass ring upon the center of it, polished to as much of a shine as the door.

Sibyl exited the cart, while Farys waited at the door. The runners, who were tanned Arokhnai youths, looked on at Sibyl's red-hued eyes with more than a little unease.

The door opened, revealing a young servant girl, whose black hair was worn in a well-oiled braid set with brass rings at regular intervals.

"Yes, Milord?" the girl asked, in the dancing Arokhnai tongue.

"I'm here for Fiss'Q," Farys said. "Tell her Farys is here, with a friend."

He glanced over his shoulder at Sibyl, who was watching.

"She already knows, Milord of Foxbridge," the girl said, opening the door wider, toward an atrium within. She rang a bell, and some porters came forth to reclaim their gear from the cart.

The inside of Fiss'Q's home was well-stocked with treasures from around the Irth: great oliphant horns mounted on hearthwood stands, exotic armors that hung like trophies on the walls, and delicate-seeming urns of jade and amalite that were, in fact, stronger than steel.

"The Mistress is in her courtyard, Milord of Foxbridge," the girl said. "I am An'Alta, if it please you. If you require anything, just let me know."

"Thank you, An'Alta," Farys said. "I'd be a liar if I didn't say I wouldn't kill for a proper bath."

An'Alta bowed. "Then we shall draw a bath for you and your lady companion."

"Perfect," Farys said, noting the nervous gaze the girl gave to Sibyl. Sibyl was occupied with gazing at some of the trophies on Fiss'Q's walls.

Farys smiled, setting down his swords. The relief he felt when the door to the street was closed was palpable. He knew that no one in Arokhnai would dare to accost the home of a Senator of the House of Shadows. In Fiss'Q's townhome, they were safe.

He turned to Sibyl, who watched him with her bright blue eyes, which now looked merely red-rimmed and irritated than they had been before, and far less terrifying.

"Shall we, then?" Farys asked, gesturing toward the courtyard. The two of them entered as one.

Thirteen

Fiss'Q was wearing a purple tunic gown patterned with gold around its edges, bound with a knot of golden cord at her slender waist. She looked as regal and pretty as Farys remembered her—flawless dark skin and ruby red eyes, her long black hair up in careful braids, with gold earrings dangling. Her mocking, fanged smile was as radiant as he remembered, and she hadn't aged a day since that night they'd spent in Forlarin, years ago.

At the sight of her friend, the Shadowlander walked over to give him a lingering embrace, her eyes on Sibyl all the while.

"Farys," Fiss'Q said. "You smell of the jungle, my dear. And you're positively basted in blood."

"It's been a trying trip," Farys said. "We met some interesting folk along the way."

"I'm sure you did," Fiss'Q said. "An'Alta will use the sun cisterns upon the roof to draw your baths. You will find my townhome to be most comfortable."

In the courtyard, there were slate pavestones and garden palms and ferns at the periphery, with marble benches and an obsidian fountain of a grinning youth who bore a cup from which the water flowed.

"Who is your friend, Farys?" Fiss'Q asked.

"This is Sibyl," Farys said.

"Of Mandria," Fiss'Q said, extending her hand to Sibyl. "You are a long way from home."

"Mandria is my home no longer," Sibyl said. "It hasn't been since I was a girl."

"Are you His?" Fiss'Q asked. Sibyl knew what she meant, and was impressed that the Shadowlander even knew of the most sacred rituals of Mandria.

"No," Sibyl said. "I have not drunk the Blood of the Dragon. I ran away before they could make me."

This pleased the Shadowlander, who nodded in silent approval.

"Most curious," Fiss'Q said. "I've known my share of Mandrians in my day, but they are all the Dragon's pawns. His Blood courses through them."

Sibyl could tell that something about it signified something to the Shadowlander, but she could not sense her thoughts and emotions the way she could sense others. To her eyes, the Shadowlander was opaque. It was a strange and unsettling sensation.

The witch and the Shadowlander regarded one another for a moment, while Farys took a seat on one of the benches, beneath the gaze of the statue at the fountain. Sibyl felt a sense of discomfort at the proximity of Farys to that statue, as if she needed to protect him from it, without knowing precisely why. For a Seer, not knowing was its own kind of thrill, and Sibyl was, for now, content to explore this.

Fiss'Q reached out, quick as a spider, and held Sibyl's face gently in her dark fingers, turning it this way and that, before Sibyl could react.

"All the same, the jungle has had its way with you, by the look of things," Fiss'Q said, letting Sibyl go before she could swat her away. "You came to me just in time, I would say."

"We were on the run," Farys said. "I felt that anybody pursuing us would be foolish to follow in the Black Jungle."

Fiss'Q again graced them with the faintest of smiles, her little fangs dimpling her lower lip. Sibyl was transfixed by this strange creature, this Shadowlander, who seemed screened from her Sight in some fashion she could not divine.

"Of course," she said. "Only madmen, monsters, and fools live long in the Black Jungle. You look almost as if the Blood Fever was overtaking you. I'm amazed they let you pass into the city, looking the way you do."

"A bloody rough journey," Farys said. "I think we both agree on that."

"Yes, of course," Fiss'Q said. "The blood magic still pulses vibrantly in Old Soria. It's ironic, really. It's as if they never truly left, isn't it?"

It had been millennia since the Sorian Empire had fallen in the Blue Plague that had ended them, brought on by a war of the gods. The reptilian overlords had been snuffed out in a massive epidemic that had left a great and gaping hole in the heart of the Irth that others had been eager to occupy.

But in the Northlands, where the Sorians had only ever been invaders and conquerors, they were more like bad memories to be forgotten. In the Southlands, where they had been at home, the memories lingered. Their presence touched everything, from the architecture, to the prevalence of their magic, to the cultural shadow they still cast. Even the masked Southlanders, who had been their imperial administrators, remained, lending their skills to new masters. The Sorians may have died out, but Soria remained.

"Where is your master, Q'rr'k?" Sibyl asked.

Fiss'Q smirked at the Mandrian witch, noting the jungle crows that had landed around the lip of her courtyard. The great, black birds looked down at them, their beady eyes shining.

"Q'rr'k hasn't been my master for a long time," Fiss'Q said.

"Is he in Arokhnai?" Farys asked. "It's our understanding that one named Valonnis, a rival of Q'rr'k's, had dealings with the Manticore long ago. "

At the mention of the Manticore, Fiss'Q's amusement dissipated somewhat.

"Ah," she said. "The Manticore."

Sibyl took her seat next to Farys.

"Is Q'rr'k here?" Farys asked.

"Ask your witch," Fiss'Q said. "Of course, she can't See him, can she? Almost no one can See us if we don't want to be Seen. I'm the only one who can find him. Which is why you came here, yes?"

"We came to see this Valonnis," Farys said. "To ask him questions."

Fiss'Q sighed, patting Farys on his wounded forearm.

"You're too late for him," Fiss'Q said. "Q'rr'k killed Valonnis a year ago. The fool attempted to assassinate Q'rr'k. I suspect it was on the order of the Manticore, although I can't prove that."

Farys glanced at Sibyl a moment before replying.

"It was to help with the Manticore, yes," Farys said. "That we learned about Valonnis having involvement

with the Manticore, well, that was something we picked up along the way."

The Shadowlander nodded.

"Why would Valonnis have helped him at all?" Sibyl asked.

"His reasons likely died with him," Fiss'Q said. "I can't speak to them, in truth. And Q'rr'k had never spoken of it, so I cannot say what he might know. He is not a bad man, although he'd probably be insulted if I said he was a good man."

Farys glanced up at the jungle crows, which were preening from their perches on the roof.

"The important thing is whether or not you'll help us find him, Fiss'Q," Farys said.

Fiss'Q leveled a lingeringly cool glance at Sibyl, then a far warmer gaze at Farys, breaking into a fanged smile.

"You know that I'd do anything you desired, Farys," Fiss'Q said.

Fourteen

After an indulgent rooftop bath, new clothes, and a proper Arokhnai feast, Farys slept for a day in the hospitable confines of Fiss'Q's townhome, and would not be stirred.

Sibyl, on the other hand, was restless after her own bath, wearing a honey-hued Arokhnai shift that made her feel out of sorts. The fabric was almost too smoothly rendered for her. It felt decadent. She worked to mend her red dress, while Fiss'Q looked on.

"Do you not like the silken shift?" Fiss'Q asked. "It's spun from threads that come from worms. A most marvelous fabric, miraculously strong and supple."

"It's lovely," Sibyl said, and shuddered at the thought of worms.

"The Market District has plentiful red fabric for you, Mandrian," Fiss'Q said. "I could send An'Alta to fetch some bolts for you, if you require them. Firmer fabric, more Mandrian in character, if you require it. She is a most adroit haggler, although I think it is mostly because people know she works for me."

Sibyl sewed with a steady hand, grateful to feel more like herself after the experience in the jungle. Her eyes were nearly themselves, again, and the visions that came were more as they should have been, instead of bleeding through her reality as they had in the jungle.

"Why would any Shadowlander help the Manticore?" Sibyl said, not satisfied with the answer Fiss'Q had given the day before.

"You're the Seer," Fiss'Q said. "Perhaps you can find that answer. If I had to venture a guess, I'd say that Valonnis saw profit in it. That would be the Arokhnai way. We can ask Q'rr'k what he knows."

"I could attempt to See what had happened," Sibyl said. "Long ago."

She didn't relish doing it after her time in the jungle, but if it helped them divine the origins of the Manticore, it would be worth it.

"I nearly lost myself in the jungle," Sibyl said.

"The Jungles of Soria can have that effect," Fiss'Q said. "You felt it, yourself, judging from how you looked when you first darkened my door. You already know all of this."

Sibyl felt uncomfortable beneath the scrutinizing gaze of this strange, lean-limbed warrior woman.

"Yes, I did," Sibyl said. "But I'm quite better, now."

Fiss'Q appeared amused by that sentiment, if only slightly.

"Rare is the magician who spurns the embrace of Sorian blood magic," Fiss'Q said. "Arokhnai deals steadily in pilgrims who make the trek. Most never return, of course. But it doesn't prevent us from indulging them in their obsession."

"I'm not a 'magician,'" Sibyl said, cutting a thread with a small, sharp knife. She worked on mending another tear.

"Of course not," Fiss'Q said. "You're a witch."

"I'm not a witch," Sibyl said. "Any more than you are an assassin."

If the stray comment was intended to wound, Fiss'Q was unharmed by it, and merely shrugged.

"I'm a Shadow Warrior," Fiss'Q said. "Some might brand me an assassin, but who are they to judge me? In the House of Shadows, I am a woman of power and influence in the richest of cities. I make my way as I am able."

Sibyl continued her stitching, feeling a measure of umbrage rising within her. The very inscrutability of the Shadowlanders was irritating to her. They were magical in a way she did not fully understand. She could sense the magic, but not its source or nature.

Had she encountered one in Mandria as a girl, she would have been terrified beyond words. That she could sit and talk to this woman in this way felt, to Sibyl, a measure of her growth since she'd left her country. She'd seen so many things since fleeing the Dragon.

"How do you know Farys?" Sibyl asked.

"Oh, we were lovers," Fiss'Q said. "Long ago. He and I, we were part of a company of warriors. Fahd, Arkhan, Sarithea, Farys, and me. We swore a blood oath to avenge one another, should someone have the audacity to slay any of us. We were very close."

Sibyl had not heard of these other people, but could imagine younger Farys, freshly wounded from the loss of his family at the hands of the Manticore, out to take on the world and strike out in his pain and anger.

"Lovers," Sibyl said.

"Yes," Fiss'Q said. "Although, if you must know, I took him. He was so young and earnest. Still very much the boy knight. Adorable. Irresistible in his indignation, his desire for justice, his pain he carries in his very soul. That hair, those eyes, that wounded heart of his. Try as she might, Sarithea could not protect him from me. The shadows will always have their way, sooner or later. Sarithea hated me for that. She probably still does, the poor thing. The Sylvanni never forget anything."

Fiss'Q seemed amused by that, chuckling.

"He is not right for you," Sibyl said. "Not at all."

"That's what made him so delectable at the time," Fiss'Q said. "The not-rightness of him. He reminded me of who I once was, before I gave my soul to the Prince of Shadows. I don't expect you, a Mandrian, to understand. Everyone knows how zealous you Mandrians are."

"I know all too well the peril of trading one's soul to a monstrous master," Sibyl said, glaring at the Shadowlander with a measure of blue-eyed reproach. Fiss'Q laughed softly.

"Sarithea's going to love to hate you," Fiss'Q said. "Oh, my, yes. She may detest you even more than she detests me. And that you're Mandrian, of all things. That will send her through the roof."

Sibyl did not know of whom the Shadowlander spoke, so she dared to use her Sight again, and could See these people of whom Fiss'Q had spoken. She was gratified that it was more as it had been before, versus the magnified Sight she'd experienced in the Black Jungle, when she Saw through everything that could be Seen.

A vision of a Sylvan woman sprang into view. Long blue hair and purple eyes. Beautifully youthful-seeming, well-dressed and well-spoken. She was a swordswoman with her own rapier, with which she pirouetted her way through battle with deadly grace. Elegant and enigmatic,

she was the first Sylvan Sibyl had sensed. She had known Farys all his life, from boyhood and beyond. She loved him dearly, and had saved his life when he was a child.

As a girl, she'd heard the stories of the wicked, sinister Sylvans, who were said to haunt the forests beyond the Red Wall, eager to snatch away Mandrian children and replace them with changelings. Sylvans were to be feared and avoided.

Sibyl had been disappointed to find none in the Forbidden Forest, beneath the shadow of the Red Mountain. The witches there professed to having no trade with Sylvans, said that their caravans were far to the east, in Imperia, and in Conradia, the Border Kingdom, and that they never strayed near Mandria.

The genteel image of Sarithea, the proud bearing and delicate beauty, was something unexpected. She was a woman of valor and true honor. Her nobility carried through to Sibyl, even through the Sight.

"Ah," Fiss'Q said, leaning in close to Sibyl. "You're using the Sight, aren't you?"

"You know of it?" Sibyl asked.

"Of course I know," Fiss'Q said. "We Shadowlanders aren't wizards—or witches—but we know the arcane arts when we see them. The magic flows around you, and the emotions that fuel it."

When Sibyl had left Mandria, she'd heard stories of Shadowlanders among the outlanders. People spoke of them in fearful whispers, these strange demons who could walk in the darkness and travel anywhere they liked.

"I've never met a Sylvan," Sibyl said. Fiss'Q smiled at this, as if the joke was on Sibyl.

"You will," Fiss'Q said. "You may be the soothsayer, but I promise you that you will. If you run with Farys, you'll cross paths with Sylvans. Sarithea won't approve of you, you know. But then, she doesn't approve of anyone who gets close to Farys."

Sibyl banished the thought of this Sarithea, turned her attention to the matters closer at hand.

"I doesn't matter. Tell me of Q'rr'k," Sibyl said. "You said he was not a bad man."

The question seemed clear enough to her, but Fiss'Q took amusement in it, waiting a lengthening moment before answering.

"Good and bad are less than meaningful to the Shadowlander," Fiss'Q said. "There is merely the opportunity or the lack thereof that guides our actions. Did Valonnis help the Manticore? Yes. Maybe he wanted Valonnis as a puppet Shadow Lord, as repayment for whatever service Valonnis had done for the Manticore in centuries past. Q'rr'k would only have seen Valonnis as an enemy, and that would be enough to damn him. Q'rr'k may not have interrogated him. I didn't see the assassination attempt, only saw the aftermath, Valonnis hung from the Courtyard of Consequences."

Sibyl didn't even want to ask what that was. She shivered, seeking to dispel the urge to use her Sight.

"Poor child. The jungle is still in your blood," Fiss'Q said. "It can become an addiction, you know."

Sibyl felt that urge, even now. It still pulsed in her veins, the sense memory of the power she possessed in those mote-soaked moments. She could feel the Harkhonites whom she turned into trees. The giddy bliss of that display of power, far beyond anything she'd ever experienced.

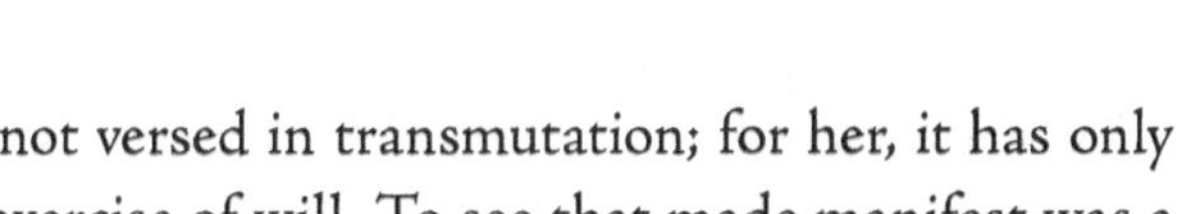

She was not versed in transmutation; for her, it has only been an exercise of will. To see that made manifest was a heady thing.

"I know it," Sibyl said. "I feel it."

"And you only felt the barest hint of it," Fiss'Q said. "Sensitive as you are, you drank deep of it, but it was still only a drink from that poison well. It's curious that the Manticore sloughed off his human skin and became the Manticore, and, yet, rather than becoming another of the menagerie of smallgods who haunt the forests of Old Soria, broke free of it and sought to carve himself an empire. It's audacious, when you think about it."

"You sound like you admire him," Sibyl said.

"Not the correct word," Fiss'Q said. "But I am intrigued by his decision. I can't hope to guess his motivations, but if pressed, I'd say that he was not content to become one god among so many other jungle gods. Rather, he sought something greater. He wanted to stand out."

"Are you talking about me again?" Farys asked, coming downstairs in an ivory tunic wrapped with a black cord at his waist.

"Yes, Farys," Fiss'Q said. "We were talking about you."

Farys yawned and stretched, shaking out his hands.

"I feel precisely three times better than I was when I first came here," Farys said. "What a marvel sleep is, yes? And not being hunted relentlessly by green-skinned Riverfolk bearing poisoned arrows and spears? Food? Drink? Good company? Better, still."

Sibyl set down her gown, rose to greet Farys, who smiled at her while he poured himself some dark red Arokhnai bloodwine into a brass cup from which he deeply drank.

"You're looking better, Sibyl," Farys said. "Can't quite say how, exactly. Ah, yes, I know: less bloody-eyed."

"You make sport of me," Sibyl said, frowning.

"Yes, don't make fun, Farys," Fiss'Q said. "Your Mandrian witch-friend was on her way to godhead, which you so rudely interrupted in your damnable insistence on dragging her to my door here in Arokhnai. A few more days in the Black Jungle, and Sibyl would have not wanted to leave, and you would not have been able to take her anyplace she didn't want to go."

Farys shrugged and drank his wine.

"I'm more persuasive than you give me credit for, Fiss'Q," Farys said. "I'd have talked her down from the firmament."

"You do have a way with words," Fiss'Q said.

"So, are we going to talk to Q'rr'k today?" Sibyl asked.

"Naturally," Fiss'Q said, glancing at Sibyl, whose blue eyes bore into her. "But if I am to help you, you must help me, as well. Let me explain...."

Fifteen

Picking through his swords, Farys had taken Aennea, his cloud-grey longsword, as his weapon for this visit to the Shadow Lord of Arokhnai, and hadn't bothered with armor, wearing only some tan leather breeches and a white cotton shirt with matching tan gloves, and his well-worn tan riding boots. He'd also brought Stillicha, on his right hip. He knew well enough how Shadowlanders fought to assume that he'd only have a moment or two available to him to attack or defend, if Q'rr'k wasn't happy to see them.

"What, no Tempest, Farys?" Fiss'Q asked.

"Tempest is resting," Farys said. "She's had her fill of late."

Fiss'Q smiled at him searchingly.

"I don't know this sword," Fiss'Q said. "It's beautiful. Dwarvish?"

"Good eye," Farys said. "Aennea is a very special blade."

He held it out for Fiss'Q, who took it and cut the air a few times with it.

"She's beautiful," Fiss'Q said. "A masterpiece. Tempest must hate her."

Farys sighed. "I wouldn't know."

She handed the grey blade back to him, and he sheathed it.

"Why don't you name your sword?" Farys asked.

"My sword doesn't need a name," Fiss'Q said. "It lives by its deeds, alone."

"It'd name it 'Nameless'," Farys said.

"Of course you would," Fiss'Q said. "Such a Borderland-ish thing to do."

Sibyl was piqued at their bantering over blades. She'd seen what Farys could do with any sword he carried, and the vagaries of particular weapons weren't things that concerned her. As much as she might appreciate the beauty of a blade, that was as far as it went with her. Besides, with her Sight, she often Saw more of the blades than they wanted to be Seen.

"Aennea is jealous," Sibyl said. "She covets your attention, Farys."

"Not the only one, I'd imagine," Fiss'Q said, treating Sibyl to a fanged grin.

Sibyl wore her mended red dress, and was more than a little concerned about their prospects for this outing. She could not be entirely sure that Fiss'Q wasn't leading them into a trap, as the Shadowlander remained as inscrutable as ever. She wore a black cloak that the ever-accommodating Fiss'Q had been kind enough to lend to her.

Fiss'Q wore a shiny black leather harness—a kind of breastplate that left her shoulders bare. She wore an aubergine, puffed-sleeve shirt and black gloves, as well as glossy black leather pants and plum-colored ankle boots. She wore her hair up in a high ponytail, bound with a cord. Her nameless sword was a magnificently strange weapon: it was a slender, two-handed sword of midnight black. The lusterless blade was as tall as Fiss'Q was, but she bore it effortlessly over her shoulder on a black leather

baldric with a gold buckle that looked like a lion biting into the leather strap.

"Ah, I see you've come prepared," Farys said.

"Of course," Fiss'Q said. "Q'rr'k may not remember the specifics of our wager. This will help jog his memory."

"Are we going to talk to him or kill him?" Sibyl asked, gazing with a degree of scorn at Fiss'Q's ostentatious attire.

"For Q'rr'k, one almost invariably leads to the other," Fiss'Q said. "If he knows we're coming, he may flee because he doesn't want to be bothered. And if we surprise him, he'll fight. So, best we fight him and subdue him in order to have a word, than ask after him and end up chasing his shadow. Now, take my hands."

She held out her hands to the Wolf Knight and the Mandrian, and they took her hands. Fiss'Q nodded, her ruby-red eyes flitting to both of them in turn.

"I shall part the Veil, and take us to the Realm of Shadow. Do not let go, or you will be lost in the Shadows. We are going to pass through the Veil and appear in Q'rr'k's domicile. He will not be happy to see you. This degree of intrusion is unwelcome to my people. But I know Q'rr'k better than any of you, and know that this must be the way, if we want a hope of him answering our questions."

Sibyl scoffed. "And you consider this man, what, a friend? A lover? A master?"

"All of the above," Fiss'Q said. "But he does not like surprises. Farys, he won't care about so much. Sorry, Farys. But you, a Mandrian? He will not like that one bit. Farys, you and I will have to...soften him up a bit. Do you understand? I will work to ensure that he does not part the Veil and flee. You will work to ensure that he does not kill the lot of us. Can you do that?"

"Naturally," Farys said.

"What will I do?" Sibyl asked.

"Do what comes naturally to you, child," Fiss'Q said. "And try not let yourself be killed. The last thing I want is the shade of a Mandrian witch haunting me for eternity."

"He won't kill me," Sibyl said, frowning at Fiss'Q. "He won't kill me at all."

Fiss'Q then concentrated, and, in the manner of the Shadowlanders, parted the Veil that separated the here and now from the there and then, and, like a fissure in the fabric of the world, Farys and Sibyl saw the breach and were guided through it by Fiss'Q, who held fast to their hands.

It was like the rest of the world receded into dancing shadow, and the light and life of the Irth faded into memory. They flitted across Arokhnai in moments, past the palaces, balconies, and promenades, the verdant gardens and merchant districts, toward the Mercenary Quarter, where the well-paid protectors of the White City laired.

And, one tower, in particular, which was Q'rr'k's tower, which faced the westernmost part of Arokhnai, looking out across the harbor and the bay, toward the salt marshes, and the mass of the Black Jungle beyond.

Into his tower they went, Fiss'Q guiding them in an eyeblink to Q'rr'k's quarters, where he drowsed in bed with three courtesans, only to jump to his feet at the sight of his former protégé appearing before him with two guests.

Fiss'Q parted the Veil once more, and the three of them were in the room with the Shadow Lord of Arokhnai, her black-skinned master, who glared at Fiss'Q with his own amethyst-eyed gaze.

"Fiss'Q, what are you doing?" Q'rr'k asked, reaching for his sword with a speed that impressed even Farys.

"Our wager, Q'rr'k," Fiss'Q said. "Remember?"

The blonde courtesans, who were triplets, screamed at the sight of the three interlopers, and ran for cover, while Farys crossed the room to try to head Q'rr'k off. At the same time, Fiss'Q drew her great black blade and charged Q'rr'k from the other direction.

Q'rr'k had reached his weapon: a curved, single-edged scimitar that bore the design of a dancing demon across its hilt, and managed to parry a cut Farys had brought down upon him with Aennea, the grey blade whispering as it sliced at the Shadowlander.

Sibyl turned her Sight upon Q'rr'k, her gaze boring into him while the courtesans ran past her in terror. It had all transpired in moments, the whir and clash of blades. Sibyl was disappointed that Q'rr'k was as immune to her Sight as Fiss'Q. She could divine nothing from him.

Q'rr'k kicked out at Farys, knocking the Wolf Knight back, and recovered himself, assuming a fighting stance, while Fiss'Q lunged at him with her greatsword, hacking his bed in half as she cut where he had been only a moment more.

"What on Irth is this?" Q'rr'k asked. "Which wager?"

"We have questions for you, My Lord," Fiss'Q asked, springing across the broken bed, only to have her two-handed downward cut blocked by Q'rr'k's upraised scimitar. Farys moved in on the Shadow Lord's flank with Aennea, cutting at him, forcing him to split his focus between his former apprentice and the Wolf Knight.

Q'rr'k laughed at them both, and made as if to part the Veil, but Fiss'Q held fast to the here and now, and did not let him cross the Veil.

"We have questions," Fiss'Q said.

"About the Manticore," Farys said.

"About Valonnis," Sibyl said.

"Fiss'Q," the Shadow Lord said. "This is hardly fair."

Farys cut at him with Aennea, the grey blade clanging as it met his scimitar in cut after cut, the Wolf Knight forcing him back, while Fiss'Q concentrated on keeping him from making good his escape.

Sibyl threw her hand back in the direction of the door through which the courtesans had fled, and brought a wardrobe down to block the door with only a thought. Seeing her for the first time, the Shadow Lord grimaced.

"You'd bring a Mandrian witch here?" Q'rr'k asked. "Here? To me? Is this an insult?"

"We have questions of you," Farys said. "Like Fiss'Q said."

Q'rr'k struck at Farys with his scimitar, the blade whistling past the Wolf Knight's jaw line, narrowly missing his throat, save for Aennea's timely parry, coming in around his guard and halting at the Shadow Lord's neck.

"I yield," Q'rr'k said. "You won our wager, darling."

At that, the Shadow Lord, let his scimitar drop to the floor, while Farys held Aennea to his neck. Fiss'Q kept the Veil shut tight, despite Q'rr'k's efforts to part it and leave them far behind. Fiss'Q looked particularly pleased, grinning at the Shadow Lord.

"A seat on the Small Council, Q'rr'k," Fiss'Q said. "As we wagered."

Q'rr'k looked exasperated, nodding.

"As promised," Q'rr'k said. Farys didn't know what Shadowlandish schemes were being hatched, and wanted Sibyl's eyes on the Shadow Lord, just in case.

"Sibyl, are you Seeing him?" Farys asked.

"Clearly," Sibyl said. Although she didn't want to tell Farys that she could See nothing of this man.

"There you have it," Farys said. "So, tell us about the Valonnis and the Manticore, Lord Q'rr'k. All that you know."

At the mention of the Manticore, the Shadow Lord almost laughed.

"Oh, that," Q'rr'k said. "Hah. You had me worried for a moment, there. Of course, I'll tell you whatever you need to know."

Sibyl was perplexed by the strange ways of the Shadowlanders. In Mandria, if someone had set upon her in this way, she would have killed them for it. But Q'rr'k seemed to think of it all as good sport.

Farys wasn't about to let his guard down with the Shadow Lord. Indeed, his bodyguards were beating on the door, demanding entry. Q'rr'k cleared his throat, addressed them.

"It's nothing, Geryonnis," Q'rr'k said. "An old friend, paying a visit. I'm fine. Stand down, on my order."

"Are you sure, Lord?" Geryonnis asked. Q'rr'k glanced uneasily at both Farys and Sibyl, and smiled at Fiss'Q.

"Quite sure," Q'rr'k said. "I'll be along in just a moment."

Then the Shadow Lord looked at them all again, uncertainly.

"I will be along in a moment, won't I?" he asked. Farys smirked at Sibyl, nodding, while Fiss'Q only held onto her fanged smirk.

"Yes," Farys said. "Provided you answer our questions."

"Ask away, Wolf Knight," the Shadow Lord said. "And you don't need to keep that cursed grey blade at my throat for me to answer. Not with that Mandrian sorceress staring holes through me."

"I'm no sorceress," Sibyl said. "Tell us about Valonnis and the Manticore."

Farys pulled Aennea away from the Shadow Lord, kicking away his scimitar, while Q'rr'k took a brass pitcher from the nightstand and poured himself some blue-hued wine, which he downed in one long swig.

"Valonnis made the Manticore," Q'rr'k said. "Not entirely. But he knew him when he was mortal. He was just another mendicant mystic from the North. We get so many down here. You know was well as I do, Fiss'Q. He came with gold and questions. Valonnis gave him answers. He didn't know who he would become. He came with gold, and Valonnis gave him a place where he could go. So many come that way. He assumed he sent him to his death, which is a suitable fate for anyone braving those jungles."

"Where did Valonnis send him?" Sibyl asked.

"He sent him to Sansibarra," Q'rr'k said. "Deep in the jungle. He thought she'd kill him. It didn't matter to him. He paid handsomely, the mad fool."

"How do you know this?" Fiss'Q asked.

"He told me," Q'rr'k said. "The night he tried to assassinate me. He told me all of it. I think he was pleased with himself, that the man he'd sent to his death into the jungle had come back as the Manticore—that he remembered him. Valonnis was always an opportunist. He likely saw a

chance for him to curry favor with the Manticore by killing me and taking over Arokhnai."

"How did the Manticore survive Sansibarra?" Fiss'Q asked.

"The Talisman of Sansibarra," Q'rr'k said. "A gift she'd given Valonnis in the past, for services rendered. It was a long time ago. The Manticore paid him a great deal of gold. It was the least he could do, giving him the Talisman. He assumed she'd simply be the end of him, and that would be the end of that. That's what one expects with Sansibarra."

"Because of what Valonnis did, he's now ravaging the Northlands," Farys said. "You've heard of that, haven't you?"

"Who hasn't?" Q'rr'k asked. "Of course, I know. As I see it, Valonnis paid for his crime. I ended him. I made an example of him, of anyone who is in service to the Manticore."

"Do you know who the Manticore was?" Sibyl asked. "Before he became the Manticore?"

"No," Q'rr'k said. "Valonnis only told me that he'd made the Manticore. That he'd come to him as a man and had emerged years later as the Manticore, and that, one day, the Manticore would come for Arokhnai, and that we would all be sent back to the Shadowlands. Valonnis was a fanatic. I can't pretend to know that man's mind. I only know that he died at my hands, after trying to usurp me."

Farys glanced at Sibyl, who nodded. "I think he speaks the truth as he knows it."

Q'rr'k looked irritated at being so interrogated, turned his attention to Fiss'Q.

"Fiss'Q," he said. "Was this really necessary?"

"You know it was," Fiss'Q said. "Would you have answered their queries if I had not?"

The Shadow Lord smiled. "Probably not. But I will not forget this."

"I told you I'd be able to beat you," Fiss'Q said.

Q'rr'k looked peevish, which, on a Shadowlander, conveyed its own kind of menace.

"You had help," he said. "It hardly counts."

"Oh, it counts, and you know it," Fiss'Q said. "We can discuss it further at the next Small Council meeting."

Sixteen

Fiss'Q sent them back the way they had come, parting the Veil and reaching her home once more, with the three of them mulling over what they'd learned from Q'rr'k. The journey through the Shadowlands had left Sibyl in particular rattled, for a Seer could See far too much in that place, which contrasted with the opacity of the Shadowlanders, themselves. The Land of Shadow, on the other hand, seemed to welcome her gaze. Farys had at least experienced it before, but, for Sibyl, it was something else. The everyday world hung pearlescent and ghostly on a sea of black, with the lives and thoughts of people fluttering in luminous torrents that assaulted the eye and the mind alike.

They sat around Fiss'Q's dining room table, in a room lit with fat white candles that hung from sconces.

"It's a ghost of this world," Sibyl said. "The essence of it, without the substance."

"Is it?" Fiss'Q asked. "It's as much my home as the Irth, now. Arokhnai is even more beautiful by Shadowlight."

Sibyl could not imagine living in the Shadowlands, or how anyone could desire to. But a runaway Mandrian could hardly find herself in a position to judge another's choices.

An'Alta had put out a meal of roast goat and wayfruit with sourbread and purple kinta bean paste, which she served with some Arokhnai goldwine.

Farys, in particular, ate heartily, while Fiss'Q nibbled and Sibyl ate sparingly. In Fiss'Q's dining room, they ate at a round bronzewood table with brass flatware on ivory-colored porcelain plates. An'Alta hovered nearby, holding a decanter of cut indigo crystal that held the goldwine.

"I'm going to pay for that at the House of Shadows. A seat on the Small Council is a highly coveted spot," Fiss'Q said. "But don't worry. Q'rr'k needs to be put in his place from time to time. If I hadn't, he'd probably have thought less of me. Besides, he'll need me on the Small Council, if the Manticore means to threaten us."

Sibyl could only shrug.

"If you are friend and ally with Q'rr'k, why would you not simply ask him for that information?" Sibyl asked. Her frustration was more than evident in the flash of her eyes and the downturn of her lip. "Why attack him?"

Fiss'Q laughed. "Ah, yes, the legendary directness of the Firstmen. Had I asked Q'rr'k, I would have been in his debt for providing the answer. But, because he had wagered that I could not possibly ever beat him at a battle of my own choosing, with a seat on the Small Council as the prize, it meant that I was able to get the information from him as a concession he owed me, which makes all the difference."

"Your people are strange," Sibyl said. "Perverse."

"I wouldn't put anything past us," Fiss'Q said, winking at her. Sibyl just sullenly ate her goat, chewing and stewing over the mannered machinations of the Shadowlandish.

"A seat on the Small Council guarantees that I'll be privy to everything worth knowing in and around Arokhnai," Fiss'Q said. "Well worth that bit of gamesmanship with Q'rr'k, I promise you."

Farys knifed the goat meat and dipped it in one of the sweet-and-savory sauces An'Alta had put out.

"So," Farys said. "Sansibarra. Do we dare confront her?"

"To what end?" Sibyl asked. "The Manticore is east and north, not west and south, with Sansibarra."

"She may have secrets to be shared," Farys said.

"I have no wish to delve into the jungle again," Sibyl said, more to herself than to him. Fiss'Q ate a stray garria fruit and mused on it.

"With me, you would not have to," Fiss'Q said. "I could take you right to her. Or as close to her as we'd dare go."

"Why not use your strange skills to transport us to the Manticore, himself?" Sibyl asked. "Put an end to him the way we could have with your master, had we wished it?"

Fiss'Q looked at Farys, who paused in his feasting to consider it.

"We could," Fiss'Q said. "We could end him today, if it was your wish. You would owe me dearly for such services, of course. I can't even imagine what you'd owe me. But the Manticore knows of us, and how to protect himself from us. We'd be foolish to think he would not be prepared."

The prospect of having his revenge on the Manticore this way was not something he had ever considered, and Sibyl could see that Farys was tempted by it.

"We could appear in his seraglio and cut him down," Farys said. "Assuming the two of us were sufficient to the task."

"The three of us," Sibyl said. "I would come, too, of course."

"Sorry, I was only thinking of the fighting," Farys said. "But he is fierce and powerful, Fiss'Q. I don't know if the two of us would be enough. He slew my father and brothers as if they were nothing."

He remembered the Manticore killing his father with his poisonous tail, and the command the beast had given to his Unhuman archers to kill his brothers in a storm of arrows fired from steel bows.

Sibyl could taste his pain. How like the Dragon the Manticore aspired to be, with his legions of warriors and acolytes, and his grand campaigns of conquest. To see him was to despise him, and all that he stood for in this Irth.

Although the Dragon was her foremost enemy, for Sibyl, by virtue of who he was, and what he had done to Farys, the Manticore was her enemy, too. She would seek his end as surely as she would see the Dragon die, as well, and her people liberated from the fervent madness the Dragon inflicted upon them all.

"However many we need, I'm sad that we couldn't talk to Valonnis directly. He knew who the Manticore had been."

"There is a way," Sibyl said.

Seventeen

The three of them had taken a boat up the Jade River the following morning, a small river runner crewed by Arokhnai sailors who were loyal to Fiss'Q. Jungle crows flocked around them, flying and cawing, making their way from tree to tree.

Sibyl was nervous, having set herself up on the bow of the sailing ship, with Farys and Fiss'Q close at hand.

"Once I get into trouble," Sibyl said. "I'll need you to whisk me back to Arokhnai, Fiss'Q. You'll know when."

"Of course," Fiss'Q said.

Farys watched Sibyl closely, as the unseen motes increasingly afflicted her. By midmorning, the blood came to her nose, by midday, her eyes, by the afternoon, her lips, as she became affected again by the fecund magic of the jungle.

The sailors looked on in dismay, while Fiss'Q looked on in interest. Beyond the boat, on the banks of the river, the Riverfolk could be seen as the white-painted apparitions they were, calling out in excitement.

"Mofasi! Mofasi! Mofasi!"

Sibyl took her seat on the deck of the boat, in her red gown, and composed herself, gave herself over to the

Sight, as drums sounded unseen in the jungle. The Sight was stronger than she ever knew it before, and she turned her gaze upon the world, and, in so doing, forgot that she was sitting on the boat at all, which became like a ghost ship to her.

"Mofasi! Mofasi! Mofasi!"

The Harkhonites' chanting was hypnotic, like breathing, their worshipful bearing feeding Sibyl, giving her greater strength still, as she sharpened her Sight, focusing it northward.

The others could see her luminous spirit. They could sense her Sensing them. The Manticore himself, in his Summer Palace at the stolen fortress city of Nikos, tended by a thousand shackled slaves, gazed skyward, aware of the intrusion from half a world away.

"You," the Manticore said, gazing through the walls of the Summer Palace, seeing her Seeing him. "The Wolf's Witch."

And she turned her bloody gaze hard upon him, past his great mane, the muscle and the sinew, the wings and poisoned tail, and saw the soul within, who he had been before.

"I would See who you really are, Monster," Sibyl said. "I would See through you."

The name of Volannis guided her search, a tether to his past. The Manticore roared at the invasion of his past, as she cut through him with her gaze.

Baern of Greenwater. Two centuries before. A scholar-scribe of the sealords of Greenwater. A bureaucrat, who stumbled upon the secret of Soria, and set out to change his fate.

The Manticore cursed her for peeling back the layers of him and knowing who he had been.

"Long dead," the Manticore said. "And long gone. I will not forgive this, Witch. I will send riders to bring you to me, and I will feast upon your Seer's eyes."

And the Manticore clapped his great, painted paws together and servants scurried to attend to him. He bellowed commands to them, to assemble his greatest hunters, who were to bring him the Wolf and the Crow, or to die trying.

"Not yet a god," Sibyl said, in wonder. "Even now. You fled too soon. Your pride and greed for conquest took you away from here too soon."

"Begone," the Manticore said, snarling at her.

"I know, now," Sibyl said, the blood tears flowing down her face, blood on her lips. "I see. This is why you fear Farys. You know. You know that he will kill you for what you have done. Fate's fury foretold."

She had his name, his true name, and what that implied. She could See his fear at this, and his determination to kill her, to take her eyes and the knowledge they carried with them.

"You and your Wolf will die so slowly," the Manticore said. "A thousand deaths await you both."

And then, all at once, she was yanked from her audience with the Manticore by a far stronger hand, one that filled her with terror, as she hovered over the Irth.

"Ah, the fledgling has left the nest at last," came the great voice, and Sibyl felt the blood flow freely down her cheeks, across her lips, as she saw the Dragon gazing at her, as it coiled over her native Mandria.

"Monstrosity," Sibyl said.

The Dragon was luminous and golden, its golden eyes the size of knightly shields, its teeth longer than lances. Its scales gave off heat, which blurred the ether around them both. Its power was beyond imagining, greater than the aura of the Manticore, and far mightier than dreadful Longmaw.

"You would do well to leave the Black Jungle, child," the Dragon said. "While you still can. The temptation to remain will blossom within you. But strong as you are, you are only a novice walking an unfamiliar path. As before, I shall send My greatest knights to reclaim you, to bring you home, where you will be made to drink of My Blood and take your proper place in My holy kingdom."

Sibyl cried her blood tears as she beheld the god-tyrant of her people, this great demon, whose gaze burned her, whose proximity carried with it a powerful price.

"I have not forgotten—nor have I forgiven—what you had done. I give you this boon, to carry with you, wherever you go: your family paid dearly for their failure. They died in pyres built for them, begging for forgiveness for your transgression. They are with Me, now, and will be, forever. Their ashes were strewn across the fields of Overwatch, returned to the Irth. Just as you must. Return to the Irth, and leave the ether behind."

And with that, the Dragon breathed white-hot ethereal fire upon Sibyl, sending her careening Irthward with a riot of images flooding her already overfilled mind—a lady knight of red and gold with a company of riders, bearing golden lances, and a blue chalice, filled to capacity, the cup running over. The roar of the Dragon, a storm-tossed island, filled with longboats, and a feral princess before a windborne banner of a black fist upon a field of white.

The Dragon's phantom fire sent Sibyl plummeting to the Irth, like a shooting star, until Old Soria loomed again into view, and the Black Jungle, and then Lake Harkhon, and, finally, to Fiss'Q and Farys, on the boat, on the Jade River.

She landed with a gasp, before falling into unconsciousness in a cascade of blood tears. Fiss'Q ordered the boat to turn back for Arokhnai, and she and Farys gathered up Sibyl, before Fiss'Q parted the Veil and whisked them back to the city, the Black Jungle looking phosphorescent in the Shadowlight as they raced back, flying over the trees, past the adoring Harkhonites, toward the luminous bustle that was Arokhnai.

"Don't you dare die on us, Mofasi," Fiss'Q whispered as they flew.

Eighteen

Three days she slumbered, the toxins of the jungle leaving her spent. Farys and Fiss'Q watched over her, and, when she finally awoke, she was mostly herself again.

"The Dragon Saw me," Sibyl said. "He's sending knights to reclaim me for Mandria. I Saw that clearly enough. A company of Golden Dragons. It's not the first time. The first time, when I was a girl, it was only three. Now, there are more. Many, many more."

Farys knew about the Golden Dragons. They were Mandria's elite knights, known mostly by repute, as they had clashed with Imperia, but had not yet contended with the Border Kingdom.

A small number of them had even gone on crusade in the Justiciar Lands in the far east. They wore golden armor and vivid red capes, bore the Dragon standard on their shields and carried long golden lances. Farys remembered seeing them as a boy, during a tourney at Foxbridge.

"A company is no small number," Farys said. "I don't think I could long stand against that many."

Fiss'Q smiled at the thought.

"Not long at all, Farys," Fiss'Q said.

"No," Sibyl said. "You would be dead. The Dragon doesn't care about you. He only wants to bring me back. We have unfinished business."

"What say we make a pact, you and I," Farys said. "You help me against the Manticore, and I'll help fight your Dragon."

Sibyl blinked away some tears and half-smiled at him. For a knight such as Farys, the Dragon was simply another thing to be slain. He had no idea what the Dragon truly was, nor how helpless he would be before Him. His willingness to dive into unknown danger on her behalf, however, was something she could hardly discount. She could See into his heart there was courage and sincerity, and that he truly meant what he said. That touched her far more than she cared to admit in the moment.

"Deal," Sibyl said. "But I fear His knights will make short work of us."

"We'll cross the Sorian Sea," Farys said. "We can head north. Make them work for it, at the very least."

"They'll not cross our paths for years," Sibyl said. "I have seen it. But they will come."

"You won't face them alone," Fiss'Q said. "I'll help you both. I'd welcome the opportunity."

Sibyl and Farys both were gratified by that, and Fiss'Q reached out for both of them, clasping her hands in theirs. Sibyl could see the sincerity in her ruby eyes, and the cool reassurance of her touch.

"What else did you see?" Farys asked, trying to keep his mind off the prospect of fighting off that many knights.

"I know the true nature of the Manticore," Sibyl said. "And his name."

"His name?" Farys asked. "What good is that?"

"It's very useful," Sibyl said. "To know a being's true name gives you power over it. I know his true name, now. And he knows this. I fear, he is sending riders after us as well."

"Now you've done it," Farys said. "A company of Golden Dragons from the west, and a horde of Unhuman mercenaries from the east. And us in the middle."

"His name is 'Baern,'" Sibyl said. "Baern of Greenwater. He is two hundred years old. I could see this. He was a scribe for the sealords who once ruled there."

"Baern," Farys said. "Oh, I imagine he didn't like you knowing that. I can't wait to call him out by his name. That'll really enrage him."

"Well," Fiss'Q said. "What shall we do, then? We're not going to insult him to death."

Sibyl could see the Manticore so clearly in her head, from when she'd visited him before. In all of his pomposity, beneath his dreadful banner of pink and gold, his thousand slave attendants with him in the Summer Palace at Nikos, the island fortress.

"We must attack him," Sibyl said. "He is not yet a god. His eagerness to conquer, perhaps, his arrogance and greed, or his own fear of his rivals propelled him from the jungles before he could grow stronger, still. He's still mortal. He can be killed."

"I like hearing that," Fiss'Q said.

"As do I," Farys said.

"We'll need an army," Sibyl said.

"Or not," Fiss'Q said. "What are you thinking, Farys?"

"No. I've seen what the Manticore does to armies," Farys said. "But we will need more swords to bring him down, I think."

"How many?" Fiss'Q asked.

"More," Sibyl said.

Farys took stock in his head, formulating a plan, while the Great Clock Tower sounded in the distance. He listened to it a long moment, counting the tolling of the bells as he formulated his plan.

"Seven. Seven swords should suffice," he said, with a wicked grin.

FINIS

A Note on the Type

The text of this book is set in Adobe Jenson Pro, an old-style serif typeface drawn for Adobe Systems by its chief type designer Robert Slimbach. Its Roman styles are based on a text face cut by Nicolas Jenson in Venice around 1470, and its italics are based on those created by Ludovico Vicentino degli Arrighi fifty years later.

Nicholas Jenson (1420–1480) was a French engraver, pioneer, printer and type designer who carried out most of his work in Venice, Italy. Jenson acted as Master of the French Royal Mint at Tours, and is credited with being the creator of one of the finest early Roman type faces. Nicholas Jenson has been something of an iconic figure among students of early printing since the nineteenth century when the aesthete William Morris praised the beauty and perfection of his roman font. Jenson is an important figure in the early history of printing and a pivotal force in the emergence of Venice as one of the first great centers of the printing press.

Ludovico Vicentino degli Arrighi (1475–1527) was a papal scribe and type designer in Renaissance Italy. He turned to printing in 1524 and designed his own italic typefaces for his work, which were widely emulated. His last printing was dated shortly before the sack of Rome (1527), during which he was probably killed.

Composed by Clever Crow Consulting and Design,
Pittsburgh, Pennsylvania

Acknowledgments

I would like to thank all of my readers, who offered their time, attention, and opinions to the writing and revision of this book. I would also like to thank Christine Marie Scott of Clever Crow Consulting and Design in Pittsburgh for her wonderful cover art and her invaluable assistance with the layout of these pages.

About the Author

Dane Vale lives in Chicago, where he conjures up Sword & Sorcery and Fantasy fiction when he's not relentlessly critiquing his twin brother's writing. He owns at least one spear, dodges drunk texts from Dionysus, and believes that there should be more megaliths in America. He cooks Italian food with verve, and has a bond with wolves and crows. His favorite cities are Knossos, Carthage, Constantinople, Venice, and Paris. **RealDaneVale.com**

Nosetouch Press is an independent book publisher
tandemly based in Chicago and Pittsburgh.
We are dedicated to bringing some of today's most
energizing fiction to readers around the world.

Our commitment to classic book design in a digital
environment brings an innovative and authentic
approach to the traditions of literary excellence.

*We're Out There™

NOSETOUCHPRESS.COM

Science Fiction | Fantasy | Urban Fantasy | Horror

Folk Horror | Occult | Supernatural | Gothic | Weird

www.ingramcontent.com/pod-product-compliance
Lightning Source LLC
Chambersburg PA
CBHW031418200726
48285CB00017BA/2470